I0561293

USA TODAY BESTSELLING AUTHOR

ALLYSON LINDT

ACELETTE PRESS

This book is a work of fiction.

While reference might be made to actual historical events or existing locations, the names, characters, places, and incidents are either the product of the author's imagination or are used fictitiously, and any resemblance to actual persons, living or dead, business establishments, events, or locales is entirely coincidental.

Copyright © 2023
by Allyson Lindt

Cover Design by Emma Rider at Moonstruck Cover Design & Photography, moonstruckcoverdesign.com
All Rights Reserved

No part of this publication may be reproduced, stored in a retrieval system, or transmitted in any form or by any means, electronic, mechanical, recording or otherwise, without the prior written permission of the author.

Manufactured in the United States of America

For my eternal dragon

PLAYLIST

Music is a huge part of my writing. Certain songs inspire scenes, capture moods, or just remind me of certain characters.

"Breathe With Me" by Lacey Sturm (feat. Lindsey Stirling)
"Alone" by Heart
"Uninvited" by BELLSAINT
"Skulls" by Halestorm
"I Can't Breathe" by Stitched Up Heart
"Conflicted" by Halestorm
"Finally Free" by Stitched Up Heart
"Natural Born Sinner" by In This Moment
"sillyworld" by Stone Sour
"Numb" by Linkin Park
"Dysfunctional You" by Shinedown

ONE

BRIENNE

When I was sixteen, my father held a *coming out* party for me. He meant it to be the type of event where he could introduce me to the wealthy businessmen he called friends, and their sons.

Instead, it was the kind of affair where he found me tucked away in a corner at the end of the night, making out with one of their girlfriends.

Sorry-not-sorry.

Tonight, I stood between the buffet table and the open bar in a ballroom in Deer Valley Lodge, and it was like being transported back ten years ago.

I sipped my drink as I watched some of the biggest names in tech investment mingle, and dine on food they would call *free* even though their money paid for it. Thank fuck they weren't here specifically to meet me tonight.

Though this was still a coming out party of sorts. Eight years ago, when I walked out of my father's house, he told me I could never come back. I hadn't.

I left the money and the lifestyle behind, and didn't leave him a forwarding address. I still kept in contact with his father—my grandfather—though. The only family I had left who mattered. One of the few people in my life who had any idea who I was, and loved me regardless.

"Hi there." A man in his mid-thirties stopped next to me, and his gaze flitted over the ink on my arms and neck, before resting on the white fabric stretched across my breasts. "I'm Jeff. Jeff Bezel."

Mostly hardware, with the occasional dive into software, similar to the company I worked for. "Hi, Jeff. Jeff Bezel." Indoctrination said *Pleasure to meet you* came next. I couldn't make myself say it, though.

To most of these people, I was no one in my everyday life. The Executive Assistant to one of the Senior Vice Presidents for Rinslet, Inc—the company throwing this party. It was how I knew who every single of them was—I'd helped stamp and seal and hand write addresses on invitations.

"Are you here with Nelon?" Jeff's gaze was still fixed on my tits.

No. Nelon couldn't pay me enough to be his date. There was probably only one couple here who I'd even consider.

"I'm Brienne. Walker."

"Walker?" Jeff raised his brows at the name. "I didn't realize Chester Jr was here. I didn't realize he'd remarried."

Gross. As in, gag me with one of those little toothpick kabobs. "I didn't either. I haven't spoken to my father in quite a while." I paused long enough to be amused by the shock on Jeff's face. "I'm here representing Chester Sr. My grandfather."

"Ah." Like that, Jeff's gaze flew to my face. Eye contact. Wow. "Pleasure to meet another board member." He extended his hand.

"I'm sure. But I'm not on the board. Would you excuse me?" I handed him my soda and turned away.

Rinslet, Inc was one of the biggest gaming companies in the world, and this annual investor party was typically the only time Grandpa made his presence known with the company. The rest of the year, he let the Chief Technology Officer and one of two co-founders have his vote, be his voice, and anything else required of a board member.

Tonight, Grandpa asked me to attend in his place. I wouldn't have agreed for anyone else, especially since I'd tried so hard for the last couple of years of working at Rinslet to hide who I was.

Getting my hair done for tonight—braiding the blond dreadlocks but leaving my bangs in curtains around my face—and dressing up in this formalwear, had me sliding into flashbacks of my father's parties.

How, even in my early teens, I was expected to look prim and proper and elegant. To mingle with his business partners and the boys they were training to take over their empires. To be a dutiful wife-to-be. Someone to marry off rather than pass the family name along to, since he hadn't had a son.

I really hated slipping into the bitterness of my past. I'd rather enjoy the free food, the occasional look of shock when people found out who I was, and maybe slip off with someone at the end of the night to fuck this stress out of my system.

Oh, and possibly send my father a photo from the bedroom of whomever I ended up with. Let him know that not only was I here and he wasn't, but I was screwing tech investors and he wasn't.

Though, his version involved less penis in the vagina and more taking their money and losing it on vaporware.

"Which kind were you? Are you?"

The question, carried on a smooth teasing baritone, startled me from my tumble into the past. Scott McAllister—the CTO my grandfather trusted with a portion of his money's future—had joined me.

Scott was enough taller than my five-foot-nine that I had to look up to meet his gaze, and I'd much rather be looking at him than almost anyone else in this room. With his dark-but-silvering, mussed hair, etched in smirk, and a muscular build that no tech exec should be allowed to have, he tended to be one of my favorite distractions.

He was also my boss every other day of the year, and happily married, so I relegated the drooling to long-distance.

"Which kind of what?" And what was the etiquette here? Did I talk to him like he was the man who signed my paychecks, or like my grandfather was the man who signed his?

Considering how hard I'd worked to distance myself from the second, the first seemed more appropriate.

Yeah, this was one of the few people I'd watch my Ps and Qs in front of.

I smoothed hands over my dress, as much to dry my palms as to make sure I looked immaculate in the white bandage dress that hugged my body and ended above my knees with a slit that ran halfway up the thigh.

He leaned against the pillar I didn't realize I'd half-hidden behind until he showed up, he and looked out at the room. "Which kind of rich kid were you?"

"Does it matter?" I wasn't any kind now. When my father disowned me, the money dried up fast. Grandpa tried to help, but I didn't let him. Making it on my own was part of proving to Dad I wasn't ruining my life by being me. These days I was an administrative assistant and working drone, like most anyone else.

Scott shrugged. "I suppose in the grand scheme of things it doesn't, but I am curious. I could guess, but people don't like it when I do that."

"Do you guess wrong a lot?" I had no idea what to make of this conversation—it was intriguing and disconcerting and I liked the way it distracted me. I was the kind of rich kid who got my first tattoo at sixteen. I was terrified that we were going to get hassled. That someone would call the cops on the underage girls. That it would hurt. But Manda already had a few tattoos, and the guy knew her. For an extra hundred bucks each, he didn't ask to see our ID when we insisted we were adults.

I'd gotten a simple heart with wings on the inside of my wrist. High enough to cover with a long sleeve, but easy enough to show off to the right people. And I loved the entire experience. The way the art looked. As we walked out of the parlor that afternoon, almost fifteen years ago, I was already planning my next tattoo.

"I almost always guess right," Scott said.

Really. That sounded like a challenge. In a fun way. "I was the weird girl all the boys wanted to talk to, because I had a tattoo, and that made me a slut." I'd been so happy they were finally paying attention to me, until I figured out that one little thing. "But I just wanted to be talking to the cute goth girl in the corner. Is that what you would've guessed?"

He raised an eyebrow. "Yes?"

"Now I'm intrigued." And enjoying this conversation. I talked to Scott on an almost daily basis, but it tended to be about when his calendar was open and if I had any questions about meeting notes.

"You're really not," Scott said.

"If you're trying to dissuade me, it's not working."

Laughter danced in brown eyes so dark they were almost black. "I would've said you were the girl who everyone thought spiked the punch bowl, but really you'd rather be at home reading than snobbing it up with whoever your father was trying to pair you with that week."

Everyone. My father had wanted to marry me to anyone who would take me—his friends' sons, then his friends when dad decided my bisexuality meant I'd be fine with anyone. "Are you speaking from experience?"

"No. I was definitely the guy who spiked the punch bowl, and the goth girl was far younger, and not at all impressed with me. But her sister was dating my best friend." He talked about it all casually, his voice amusement mingled with apathy.

This was a far better way to remember my past than drowning in suffocating memories. "You're not drinking tonight."

"You noticed."

"I know what everyone in the room is drinking. Makes a night safer." The night my tattoo was discovered, My father had waited until all the guests were gone, and approached with anger flashing on his face.

"What did you do?" His voice had been harsh. He grabbed my arm hard enough for me to yelp, and yanked up my sleeve. "What the fuck is this? You're not a cheap whore."

The words clawed under my skin and a lifetime of repressed frustration snapped the dam I'd built to hold it all in. "You're right, I'm not. I'm a high class escort, and you're my pimp, trying to sell me to the highest bidder."

I still couldn't believe I'd said that, but I also couldn't believe I'd waited so long. That was the first night I'd screamed back, but it wasn't the last. My retorts grew bolder and more honest as time went on. As more of his friends hit on me, rather than pawning me off to their sons. As more of them groped me in back corners. The drunk ones were harder to shrug off than the sober ones, so I learned to watch, as my father told me to politely put up with it, and burst a blood vessel with every new tattoo I got in retaliation.

"Am I interrupting?" A pleasant voice asked.

I'd only met Kenzie a few times, but everyone at

7

work knew she was the boss's wife. And she was as fun to look at as he was.

"Not at all. We're just bonding over our shared trauma." Scott wrapped an arm around her waist and pulled her closer. On the surface, they were picture perfect. Straight out of an episode of *Housewives of...*

The muscle-bound billionaire and his younger, blond and sexy trophy wife. Appearances were deceiving, especially in their case. From everything I'd seen, they were loving together. Sweet, and good people.

Not that I had any idea what their life was behind closed doors, though rumors said it included an open marriage. And had I ever found their faces slipping into my threesome fantasies? Only on a regular basis.

"You two have met formally, haven't you?" Scott asked. "Kenzie, this is Brienne. Bri, this is Kenzie."

"I know," I said. "Nice to see you again."

Kenzie's smile was warm and sweet, with a hint of spice underneath, like fresh cinnamon rolls. "You too. You work for Chloe, don't you? I didn't realize you were..." She glanced around the room.

"She's Chester Sr's granddaughter," Scott explained.

I'd gotten the job based on my own merits, and I wanted to be treated like everyone else. "Grandpa asked me to attend on his behalf."

"I'm sorry he's not here, but I'm glad you are." Unlike anyone who had offered a similar sentiment, Kenzie sounded like she meant it. "Are you enjoying the evening?"

I wasn't much for holding my tongue, unless the conversation was getting personal. "Does anyone really enjoy an evening like this? All the pomp and circumstance and bullshit... Though bonding over the shared childhood trauma was nice, I guess." I snapped my jaw shut when I realized Scott was staring at me with wide-eyed disbelief.

"What are you doing? Don't tell her that." His tone held an edge that sliced through me.

Did I miss something?

Kenzie smacked his chest lightly. "Knock it off. Look at her, she doesn't know you're joking."

"I am." Scott smirked. "Joking, that is. I'm only here because Kenzie makes me be here, and she knows it."

Thank God. "I have a hard time believing you do anything because someone else tells you to, and isn't this *your* party?"

"Marriage is about compromise. And no. This is *their* party." He gestured at the room. "They can't make me do much as long as I don't lose their money, but I try to keep the wallets happy as long as their requests are reasonable."

I liked his directness. "As for me, I've done my time for the night. I was about to take off."

"Don't say that." Kenzie sounded disappointed. "You'll give him ideas."

"I don't think he needs any help with that." Okay, so tonight had one advantage—for the moment I was equals with Scott instead of a peon.

Scott grinned. "I don't." He pulled his phone from his suit coat pocket and glanced at the screen. "I need to greet our adoring fans. Bri, do me a favor and keep my date company?"

"Yes, sir."

He walked away, and I turned to Kenzie. "Do we find a table now, or…?" I was required to be at all of my father's parties when I was younger, but never allowed to stay for the financial presentations. I didn't need to know those kinds of things—my husband would take care of all of that one day.

Not that I'd ever complained, but at this moment it left me feeling out of place.

TWO
KENZIE

I'D NOTICED BRI BEFORE——SHE WAS THE GORGEOUS
woman with the stunning tattoos along her arms and
legs, who was hard to miss. But I'd never had an excuse
to linger and talk.

Now I was leading her to a table, so we could listen
to the Rinslet financials.

I doubted I'd be paying much attention to the
presentation, though. I already knew most of the information, and it was so difficult for me to pull my attention away from Bri. I was both infatuated with her look
and envious of her boldness. If she didn't work at
Rinslet, I'd be considering hooking up with her.

About a year ago, after a lot of talking, Scott and I
opened our marriage. At least partly because I wanted
to explore my bisexuality in a way I'd never been
comfortable with when I was younger. Neither of us
acted on the opportunity much, thanks to busy sched-
ules. I'd gone out with a couple of women, and Scott

and I had one threesome that was as awkward and terrifying as it was new and sensual.

We were quiet about the whole *we can see other people* aspect of our lives, because it didn't take long to get tired of hearing *you two won't last if you do this* and *there must be something wrong with your marriage*.

There was nothing wrong with my marriage, but I did have a problem with the awkward silence that settled between Bri and me now that Scott was gone, and we were seated. I had no idea how to start a conversation with a woman who had matched him quip for quip and never flinched.

Scott stepped up to the podium at the front of the room, and his friendly greeting rang out through the sound system. Even in a room full of wealthy businessmen he wasn't somber. His brashness had embarrassed me when we first met. I'd wondered how he could draw so much attention in all the wrong ways.

These days it didn't usually matter to me. I loved him for his boldness.

He slid into his introduction and presentation without pause. Despite his irreverence, he knew his audience and he knew what to say to capture their attention. In this case it was a fast-paced version of *this is how we're making you money*.

"How many times over have you heard this speech?" Bri asked.

I wasn't sure what to make of the question, since the presentation changed every year. "I don't understand."

"Does he rehearse all of this with you, or someone else?"

I laughed lightly. "Scott doesn't rehearse. He knows the important numbers—good memory—and the rest is ad-libbed. Isn't it sexy?" Why did I ask her that?

Her silence made me think Bri wondered the same thing. "If your boss asks *are you busy*, how do you answer?" she replied.

"The ultimate trick question." Saying *yes* meant blowing off the person in charge and saying *no* implied one wasn't doing anything at work.

"I always thought it was too, but I've just changed my mind. Apparently his wife asking if he's sexy is a far trickier question to navigate."

My smile grew. "I promise I'm not trying to trip you up."

"The two of you make a gorgeous couple."

I raised an eyebrow. "Quite the diplomatic answer. Did you learn that growing up?" I teased.

"Never tell anyone I learned things like that from my childhood." Her tone was light. "I mean the things I say. If this were a different kind of party…" She shook her head. "Never mind."

Interesting. "You can't drop a sentence like that and think you can get away with not finishing it. What kind of party, and what would you do?"

"The kind of party a woman doesn't admit she attends, especially when she works in tech and lives in a conservative state."

She means an orgy. The answer nipped at my thoughts, but I hated to assume. "A Tupperware party?"

Bri laughed. "Can you imagine me buying Tupperware?"

"Sex toys?" That was closer to what I didn't dare think, but not quite there. The answer I really wanted to say rested on the tip of my tongue, but if I spit it out and she was offended, the night could be over.

Bri scrunched up her face. "I mean… technically, yes?"

It wasn't proper for me to push, but I wanted to know more about her, and heat was spilling through me, prompting my imagination to tumbled down the *sex party* rabbit hole. "You work at Rinslet, so you've heard the stories about the early days." In other words, the orgies.

"Do the stories bother you?" Bri was definitely diplomatic in some things, regardless of her insistence to the contrary.

"The stories fascinate me. The only thing I get hung up on is that Scott never participated, so he doesn't have any graphic details to share." Oh gawd, did I really just admit that? I'd never told anyone that except Scott, not even my sister. What was happening? "At least he had a sense of propriety when it came to employees, right?" Could I stop talking now, please?

Bri looked amused. "To your question, yes, *that* kind of party."

Hot. "You've been to…"

"An orgy or two, yes." Despite her initial reluctance to answer, when she got there she spoke without hesitation. "Not that I make a habit of it."

It didn't matter because my imagination was already racing ahead to fill in the blanks. Fantasizing about watching Bri naked with someone else. With me. With

Scott. My pulse hammered in my ears at the images. "What was it like?"

Bri bit her bottom lip. "There are a lot more rules than normal sex, especially when it comes to consent. But..." She drew in a long breath, and my gaze froze on the rise and fall of her chest. "If you like watching or being watched or tasting multiple people in a single night and fantasizing about who they've been with... I had fun."

The idea of any and all of those things had me breathing shallowly. "Which one are you?" How did we get on this topic? I shouldn't be pursuing it, but I couldn't think of anything else.

"All of the above. I guess I'm just a deviant."

"Nothing wrong with that."

Bri chuckled. "By definition, there's something very wrong with that."

"You can't believe everything you read in books." Like dictionaries? Who was I that I was ignoring propriety to keep up this conversation?

Bri pouted. "No? Then I should stop waiting for my invitation to Hogwarts?"

"Sorry." This was so easy. So much fun.

"Hang on." Bri held up a finger and cocked her ear toward the podium. "What did he just say?"

I'd only half been listening to Scott. I knew most of what he was going to talk about, despite not having heard him rehearse. "Something about the Nashville project."

She snapped a few photos of the stage then typed something on her phone.

"What was that?" I asked.

"Don't know. I just hadn't heard it and it seemed important."

I didn't think it was any more relevant than anything else he'd shared, but I was viewing this entire event through a different lens.

We slid back into the conversation, but the orgy topic didn't feel appropriate anymore. I lost track of the rest of the room, until I looked around and didn't see nearly as many people as were here before.

Scott rested a hand on my back, and kissed me on the cheek. "Sorry to be gone so long." He sounded drained. He loved mingling, but not under these circumstances.

"You had work to do. Bri kept me company," I said.

Scott's smile was tired too. "Perfect. Are you ready to get out of here?"

I wasn't. I didn't want the night to end with Bri, and I was torn between taking my husband home and staying and flirting with the cute new girl.

THREE
SCOTT

"I SHOULD GET GOING TOO." DESPITE BRI'S WORDS, SHE didn't push back from the table.

When she finally stood, Kenzie frowned.

I'd approached Bri tonight because I recognized her and the feeling-out-of-place expression she wore. And because she looked incredible in a white dress that hugged all her curves, and showed just enough skin to make her look temptingly lickable and like a lot of fun to unwrap.

Not that I'd ever hit on someone who worked for me. I liked to embrace my don't-give-a-fuck public persona, but there were distinct lines I didn't cross. I had with Kenzie, when she was my PR person, trying to clean up said public persona, but there was no reason to push my luck that way ever again.

Though, if Kenzie were to… That was a degree removed from me and didn't count, right?

What was going on with my head? Recognizing

someone was attractive was a huge step away from imagining her with my wife. I needed to stop.

"We'll walk you out," I said to Bri.

I'd caught glimpses of the women chatting during my presentation, but whatever they'd had to say had died now that I was here. Neither of them said much of anything as we grabbed our coats and made our way toward the exit.

We stepped outside into a night almost as bright as day, thanks to more than a foot of fresh snow.

"Gorgeous." Bri's voice was soft and filled with awe.

She really was, and I wasn't the only one watching her. Though, I needed to stop.

"You're not driving home in this, are you?" Kenzie asked.

We held the meeting in Park City, up in the mountains, so our guests could hit up late-in-season skiing at the same time. Kenzie and I had already planned to spend the weekend in our house up here, and now I was grateful. Driving those hills in fresh snow wasn't fun.

Bri nodded. "I don't have much of a choice, unless I want to sleep in my car."

"No. You're staying with us, at least for tonight. We'll reevaluate in the morning." I couldn't have Kenzie's new friend, one of Rinslet's best Executive Assistants, driving home in bad weather.

Bri worked her jaw. I was prepared to push the issue if she argued. I didn't like hearing *no* when I'd made up my mind.

"He's right." Kenzie sounded kinder about her insistence. "We have a guest room, you won't be imposing. Plus, we can keep talking."

"It's just…" Bri nudged the snow with the toe of her white heels. "Going back to the boss's condo…"

"I promise we never do anything untoward with the stunning women we bring home, unless they beg." What the fuck was I doing?

The pink on Kenzie's cheeks wasn't just from the cold.

"Do you bring a lot of stunning women home?" Bri asked.

Kenzie shook her head. "He's making us sound like serial killers."

"He wasn't, but now that you mention it…" Bri's tone was light.

This was going to be so much trouble. "It's a spare room, during a snowstorm." Even though I'd started it, apparently I had to end it, too. "You're both perverts and sickos."

"You know you love it." Kenzie had found her voice.

Fuck. Was I going to have to behave if we did this? I really hated to rein myself in. "You're not wrong."

Fortunately the valet chose that moment to pull up with my SUV. He opened both passenger doors, and Bri hesitated.

"Get your car in the morning," I said. "No arguments. The roads aren't safe."

Bri gave a brief nod, and climbed into the back seat, while I exercised zero restraint in watching the way her dress stretched and shifted with the movement.

I shoved any unformed thoughts aside and turned to

find Kenzie watching me. She raised her brows, and her mouth was twisted in question and amusement.

I shook my head, not sure if I was saying *we'll talk later* or *don't worry about it*, and brushed my lips over hers before nudging her into the vehicle.

The party atmosphere we'd left behind had reminded me too much of when I was younger. My father's associates. Did Bri have similar flashbacks? She didn't tell anyone who she was, but I knew her father. If tech execs had rivals, I was pretty sure I was his.

His father—Bri's grandfather—sat on my Board of Directors, and had given me his vote and voice. As far as Chester Jr was concerned, I'd stolen his birthright.

The drive back to the mountain house was silence amplified, with the snow muting the outside world and conversation stalling while I navigated unplowed roads with a white-knuckled grip on the steering wheel. What should've been a ten minute drive took more than thirty, and I could taste my relief when we finally pulled into the garage.

This place was far too big for two of us, or even three of us, but it made a great spot for retreats or team building—also known as filling the rooms with laptops, and spending the weekend with a group from Rinslet slaughtering each other in first person shooters.

Kenzie gave Bri a brief tour from where we stood, pointing out the guest room, the master suite, important things like the kitchen, and ending with, "Let us know if you need anything."

"I need to know what that is." Bri pointed at the

display shelf that covered one living room wall, and walked toward it.

When I realized it was the erector set box that caught her attention, I grinned. One of my favorite pieces in the room.

"What is it?" Bri was focused on the watch inside. "Like, an early Apple watch design?"

"It's just a prop." I joined her.

Kenzie did as well, shaking her head. "It's not *just a prop*. It's one of the original two way communicators from *Mission: Impossible.*"

"*Original* original?" Bri reached a hand out, but didn't touch the watch or the box. "Like the old TV show?"

Kenzie nodded and dug into her purse. "Scott got the watch for me at a Konsoles for Kids auction a few years ago. I used to watch reruns of the show and I loved it."

Seeing her light up talking about something so simple made me smile. I'd been attending the auction—an event that raised money for children's hospitals—for years. But they meant more to me since I met Kenzie.

"What's with the dopey look?" Bri was watching me. She glanced at Kenzie and back at me again. "It has to do with her, doesn't it?"

Most of the time my dopey looks had to do with Kenzie. "Good memories of a few weeks after she and I met. I had no idea if she was even going to show up."

"I told you I'd be there." Kenzie pulled something from her purse.

"But you were also mad at me," I said.

She shook her head. "Because you were being an asshole. I was within my rights."

"Kind of like getting mad at a table for being a table." Bri shrugged.

I liked her. I laughed both at the comment and Kenzie's shock. "She showed up, though. Complete with makeup to give her gray skin, a short top and skirt, and looking like the most gorgeous fucking drow queen I'd ever seen." Yeah, that was an incredible memory. "If I hadn't already been hooked on Kenzie, that night would've sunk me."

"I wish I could've seen that." Bri almost looked wistful.

This was different. Weird in the best kind of way. She didn't hold back on most things, and I wasn't used to that with people. It was what took her from being just another pretty face to being a fascinating individual.

"If you love the watch, you have to see this." Kenzie held up the remote pulled from the drawer under the display. She pressed one of the buttons, and the box the watch was in closed slowly. "Scott built the display case and tweaked the remote software so I could control the lid without touching it."

"No shit? I knew people did that, but I've never seen it. May I?" Bri leaned in. "Linux?" She looked at me.

This was my kind of conversation. "Mostly. Proprietary flavor, similar to what sits at the core of our rendering engine. It can extrapolate—"

"Hang on." Bri held up her hand. "You're going to lose me in about negative two-point-five seconds."

I stared back, one eyebrow raised. "You make small talk about Linux?"

"I make small talk about a lot of things. Good training." She winced, but it vanished so quickly I might have imagined it.

"What do you make *big* talk about?" I asked.

Kenzie slapped me lightly on the arm. "Be nice."

"You mean *be polite*. I'm being nice."

Bri laughed. "I make big talk about a lot of things too. The watch? Super sweet story. The box and remote? Amazing, even if I don't understand the details of the tech."

"Isn't it, though?" Kenzie's mood shifted toward bright.

"It's like an episode of Voyager or Farscape or something," Bri said.

Now she was really speaking my language. And Kenzie's. The reference was random, but I knew exactly where she was going with it. "Where it's obvious the characters are from two different worlds, but one of them gets the other this perfect tie to their past—"

"And they curl up and watch movies together and have popcorn." Kenzie finished for me.

Bri snapped. "*Exactly*." She frowned and looked around her, panic spreading across her face. "We're not trapped in a TV show from the past, are we? Where's the laugh track?" She was funny.

I liked it. "Nah. If this were a TV show, one of us would've spilled our wine by now. Probably the boss, on his VP's assistant's white dress. Biggest potential for heartache and television angst there."

"Really hoping it's not TV. Because that means this ends in"—Kenzie checked her watch—"seven minutes, and tomorrow, it's like this never happened."

"Boo." Bri frowned. "But I bet you look really cute in your network TV appropriate pajamas." She clamped her jaw shut.

Nope. I wasn't letting her clam up now. We were beyond the *pretend we like being appropriate* point. "She does. I promise you, no one makes flannel look sexier." Bri might. Or, not sexier, just a different kind of sexy. And both of them together...

Kenzie blushed, growing even pinker when Bri looked her over.

"I can picture it now." Bri caught her bottom lip between her teeth.

I wasn't going to wonder what it would be like to taste those lips. To watch Kenzie taste them. To share—

This was surreal. Even more than being trapped in a TV show. Even if Bri was off limits, watching her flirt with Kenzie was definitely working for me.

Bri cleared her throat. "Speaking of how things work on TV... I should disappear to my own separate bed. Thank you for letting me stay tonight." The polite mask that slipped in made my thoughts growl in distaste.

"I'll grab you something to change into." Kenzie was on her feet in an instant. "Come with me."

Only if you time it right.

Apparently there were some things I knew better than to say in polite company.

FOUR

KENZIE

Tonight definitely didn't end the way I expected.

There was a pretty, smart, funny woman across the house. The kind of woman I both wished I could be, and could easily picture myself being with.

Knowing that being with her was unlikely didn't stop the fantasies from filling my head. Especially since she'd told me she'd been to sex parties.

Orgies.

I was still imagining what she tasted like. Soda and violet lipstick? Would she let me bury my face between her legs? I bet she knew how to do amazing things with her fingers. It was almost terrifying the way my mind was racing around thoughts of her. I usually had a lot more control.

The instant Scott closed the bedroom door, shutting him and me off from the rest of the house, I draped my arms around his neck. "I want to play," I murmured against his mouth.

His raised eyebrow was the only hint he gave that he

was surprised to see me initiating. "You mean you want to fantasize about a pretty girl eating your pussy."

The direct words made me flush with heat. "I can do that by myself. I want you." It took me a long time to learn how to be up front about what I wanted from Scott, and it wasn't something I did with anyone outside the bedroom. But something about Bri tonight loosened my tongue...

He dragged his hands up my arms to grab my wrists, spun me so my back was to the doorframe, and pinned my hands above my head. "Uh-huh."

"I can't have her." I exaggerated my pout.

"So I'm your pity fuck?" His voice was a low growl, but he wasn't upset. He tightened his grip, his fingers digging into the tendons in my wrists. The roughness wasn't new for us, and he'd stop if I asked him to.

I wouldn't. "Never."

"Damn right." He moved his free hand to my breast to knead. To pinch, and roll my nipple through fabric, until my breathing was jagged and I was squirming against the way he restrained me.

Scott let go and stepped back. "Clothes off. Except the stockings."

I made a show of unzipping my dress, and letting it slide down my body. Pushing my panties to the ground, but not touching the thigh highs, held in place by garters. I kicked the clothing aside, and basked in the way he devoured me with his gaze.

"Are you still thinking about her?" Scott caught my wrists again, yanking them behind me as he pressed his hard body to mine.

I was. Bri captivated me in a way few could. A few years ago, I would've been scared to admit that I was attracted to another woman. Especially after I was married. "Yes." I liked being able to say that aloud.

"Imagining her between your legs." Scott wedged his leg between my thighs and pressed his knee to my mound.

Oh, geez. If I shifted my weight, if I slipped against him just right… "Yes."

He lowered his mouth to my neck, to kiss and suck along the tender flesh. To bite hard enough to mark me. "Do you wish she was the one doing this right now?"

Yes. No. Maybe. Was there a right answer? He raised his leg higher, applying more force to my core, and I ground against his thigh. Words were too hard, and the best I had was a moan.

The harder I rode him, the more orgasm flitted just out of reach. When he moved his attention to my breasts, biting lightly at my nipples and kneading hard, every inch of my body lit up. Climax spilled through me, and I lost myself in the pleasure.

I wanted to cry out, but we did have a guest.

If I screamed, would Bri know what we were up to? Would she join us?

Scott never let go of me as he pulled away. He kept me upright, despite my wobbly legs, and guided me to the bed. With a playful shove, he pushed me back onto the mattress, then undid his trousers and worked his cock free.

I pressed my toes to his chest to stop him, when he tried to crawl up my body.

"Clothes off," I said.

His smirk sent a fresh wave of shivers rushing over me. "Don't want me to ruin the suit?"

I looked at his leg, slick with my juices, and pursed my lips. "Too late for that. No. I want to feel you."

"I can do that." He stripped out of his jacket while I watched. Took his time unbuttoning his shirt and slipping it off. A short while later, he was naked, and urging me farther onto the bed.

He forced my legs apart again, and thrust inside me without warning. The sex was hard and fast. Frantic in a way it hadn't been in a while. It was the kind of pounding that would linger through morning, and it felt so good to have him slamming against me. Grunting, and devouring my gasps with kisses.

And when he spilled inside me, there was a release that was more than physical. There was a connection that tied us together and reminded me of so many of the things I loved about this man.

The fantasy of Bri should be enough. Mostly because she worked for him, and if I was going to be with her, I'd want this kind of intensity.

How horrible was I, thinking about someone else with my husband inside me?

He brushed his lips over mine and rolled to the side, taking me with him. We lay in silence for a while, catching our breath and enjoying the closeness.

"You know, if you were to… With her." Scott was uncharacteristically vague. "I don't have a problem with that."

I knew that, and it was another thing that made him wonderful.

I wanted to. I wanted to go explore all sorts of things with Bri. To discover things about myself that had been out of reach, even with the couple of women I'd been with.

At the same time, a sliver of fear reminded me that if I did that, I could never go back.

FIVE

KENZIE

Scott's voice reached out to my half-conscious brain, and my body reacted in a rush of heat before my mind caught up. He used that tone specifically in the bedroom.

No.

The reality stopped my desire before it could run away with itself. That wasn't the *take off all your clothes so I can fuck you* voice, it was the *why did you call me on a Saturday morning with a work problem this stupid* voice.

Oops.

His hours had never been an issue for me. I knew coming into this relationship that he was a hands-on executive who'd put in countless days and nights to build the empire he and Zach had created. Scott's work was as much passion as it was a job.

But lately the spark was missing. He scowled more than he smiled, and this morning there was an undeniable growl to his voice.

If I closed my eyes and stayed in bed a little longer,

listening to his tone more than his words, could I still pretend they were sexy words? The longer he talked, the happier he sounded, so it was a distinct possibility.

His footsteps were a consistent but soft beat on the throw rug. He always paced when he was thinking, and the sound was comforting, until it was joined by the *snick* of the door opening.

I was on my feet in an instant, as if I'd been thrown from the bed, and I grabbed his arm before he could walk out of the bedroom.

He gave me a puzzled look.

I pressed my mouth to his free ear. "We have a guest."

He smirked. The bastard actually looked like he was considering the consequences of wandering into the house naked.

I raised my eyebrows.

He rolled his eyes and reached for a pair of sweat-pants, to tug those on before leaving. The entire exchange, he never stopped spitting out programming jargon to the person on the other end of the line.

I dressed quickly, and followed him so I could make coffee and see if Bri needed anything.

She was already up, sitting on the couch with a book in her lap. Rather than reading though, her gaze was glued to Scott.

I could be jealous, or I could use her distraction as an excuse to watch her. The latter sounded far more productive. Besides, I didn't blame her for looking—he did illicit things, possibly illegal things, to those sweat-pants. Especially since he was shirtless.

There had never been a time in Scott's and my relationship where other women hadn't checked him out, but this was different. There was a spark with Bri and me last night. Now that the heat that had driven the frantic sex with Scott had faded, reality set in. Was exploring with her even an option, given who she was? Who we were?

"Did you sleep all right?" I asked her softly.

She looked up, eyes wide like a deer caught in the headlights, and gave a quick shake of her head. Like she'd flipped a switch, gawking turned to a neutral smile. "I did, thank you. I hope it's all right that I snagged this off the shelf in your guest room." She held up my well-worn copy of *Neuromancer*.

"Of course. As long as you're kind to Mr. Gibson's words."

Bri hugged the book to her chest, an exaggerated look of offense on her face. "I would never harm an innocent book."

I definitely liked her. "Do you want coffee?"

"I would *love* that. Lots of cream and sugar?"

I grinned. "Just the way I like it. I'll be back."

I returned a few minutes later with a pot of coffee, three mugs, and sugar and cream, all balanced on a tray. Being a proper hostess was always important.

Scott had dressed while I was gone, though the battered jeans and T-shirt as old as his company were a stark contrast to what he'd worn to the party last night. This was the real Scott. The man who cared more about code and creativity than pandering to investors, and who made people love him just by existing.

It had worked on me.

He was sitting next to Bri on the couch, twisted toward her with one leg on the couch and his arm draped over the back.

She was laughing. "I don't know. Is *nut* butter really better than *ball* butter?"

"I guess it all depends on how much pineapple juice he's had to drink." Scott stood abruptly. "Don't move." He pointed at Bri.

Why did him using the Boss Voice on her send a shiver of desire racing up my spine?

For the first time since seeing my husband talking to Bri last night, my jealousy was real and tasted sour.

"Coffee. You're a literal angel." Scott paused long enough to brush his lips over mine, before he strode toward the master bedroom.

I set the tray on the table and stole Scott's spot next to Bri.

"Oh, my God. Thank you." Bri grabbed a mug of coffee, prepped it, and took a sip. "You two have been great. I don't know how I'll repay you."

"No need." It was an easier answer than picking between *kiss me? Let me see what it's like* and *stop flirting with my husband*.

That was bitchy of me.

Scott was back a moment later with his laptop. "I have to head out to Nashville, Kenz." He said as he approached us. "They need things I can't do over the phone."

"How long?" Though I was used to his work hours, I didn't like when he traveled. It was a dumb thing, but living with him had gotten me hooked on waking up next to him. I hated sleeping alone.

He shook his head and crouched on the floor behind the couch, to set his laptop between Bri and me. "At least through the weekend."

"Okay." It was what it was, but I didn't have to look forward to it. The first several trips he took, I'd gone with him. But he didn't tend to have any free time on the road, and I'd shopped myself to death and then some. So most of the time now I stayed home.

Scott opened his laptop. "Okay, this is the new stuff from Art." He struck a few keys and clicked the trackpad a few times, and images loaded on the computer.

"The *Top Secret* stuff?" Bri spoke with a reverent sort of excitement.

"Exactly." Scott loaded a short demo video.

I'd seen this a few times. Scott was pleased with it, not only because it showed off multiple facets of what Rinslet could do, but because he'd sneaked in some time to help build it. Any time he got to create, it made him happy, and he didn't do enough of it anymore.

This gave me the opportunity to watch him instead. And Bri. To listen to their back and forth. The work lingo. The slang and acronyms that came easily to both of them, because they talked like this every day.

The envy was back, but it wasn't the bitter jealousy that was there when I walked out of the kitchen. She was a part of a world he loved. A piece of something I would never belong to.

It was a random thought, and I didn't like the weight

that came with it. But it was also the kind of thought that had been niggling me more and more lately.

Before I met Scott, I was in PR, and few were better at it than I was. These days, I offered similar services for charity groups, and I loved that work, but I wasn't *part of* anything.

Those were thoughts for me to deal with, not to heap on them. As Scott closed his laptop, I forced a neutral expression and state of mind into place.

Scott looked at me. "I need to run. Do you want me to drop you off at home?"

I wasn't quite ready to leave yet. "I can call a car."

"I can take you home later.," Bri said.

Like that, I felt better. Why?

Because even though I had to give up Scott for a few days, and that weird *what am I good for* feeling gnawed at the back of my mind, I got to spend more time with this fascinating woman. "I'd love that."

"Perfect." Scott tugged me to my feet and wrapped an arm around my waist. His kiss was hard enough to make my toes curl and erase the last of my intrusive thoughts. When he broke away, he pressed his lips to my forehead. "I'll text you when I land. Try to do at least one thing I would."

I couldn't help but smile at that. Could Bri help me figure that out? "I'll try."

Not that propositioning Bri was a good idea, and I had zero clue how to be the aggressor, but that didn't stop the fantasy from whispering through my mind of kissing her. Doing more.

When Scott left, I found something for Bri to wear

so she and I could go out to breakfast. She was a few inches taller than I was, but had a similar build, and she wore my clothes with a kind of reckless majesty I could only dream of pulling off.

We had an Uber drop us off at Park City Main Street, because it was easier than driving ourselves through skier-clogged streets.

"This place has the best pastries," I said to Bri as we strolled down a side alley, and appeared on the busy street. "Oh." The line was out the door and stretched past the building next to it. Apparently the secret was out. "We can go someplace else."

"No way. Not after the build-up you gave their croissants. Unless you have places you need to be."

"I don't. I'm perfectly happy here." I hoped she would read into that. It seemed my resolve to not get involved with the woman from my husband's office was rapidly slipping away. Who was I that I thought breakfast constituted the potential for more?

Bri hooked her arm through mine and tugged me into the line. "Me too. Me neither? Other way around."

The line moved quickly, which was good because the press of people made conversation difficult, but disappointing because when we stepped inside, Bri let go of me. A table had opened up in the back corner of the dining room.

"I'll snag us a seat," Bri said. She gave me her order, then cut through the crowds Moses parting the Red Sea.

As I inched the last few feet toward the register, I tried to force my gaze to wander. To not stare at the stunning woman holding a table for us. Snippets of the past wove into the present, taking me back to the first day I met Scott.

I'd been trying to prove to myself that I was bold, that I could be as outgoing and fun as my twin, Riley. So that day I'd approached the sexy guy in a crowded coffee shop and asked if I could share his table.

Today would be the perfect day to rediscover that boldness, as long as I could quiet the flutters of anticipation in my belly.

I finally made it to the front of the line, placed our order, and carried our food and coffee to the table where Bri waited.

"Mmm... More coffee." She took a sip of hers. "Guaranteeing I won't need to sleep until Monday." Her tone was light.

But the reminder of sleeping alone passed a cloud over my mood. "I like the sound of that."

"Are you all right?" Bri asked.

Did I let an emotion show that I shouldn't have? Crap. "I'm fine. Having a lot of fun." My smile was genuine.

"Okay." She looked less than convinced. "I do think it's sweet that you miss him when he's gone."

"Don't most spouses?"

"Not in my experience. I like seeing people who actually care about each other."

I liked being cared about. When Scott and I first talked about seeing other people, I struggled with the idea of how much I loved him, but still wanting to sleep with someone else. There were still times when I wondered if I was doing something wrong—feeling something wrong—but I knew what he was to me, and that I was capable of feeling for him and others at the same time.

"Can I ask you something personal?" Bri's tone shifted toward more subdued.

Did it get more personal than me all-but asking her last night if she'd been to sex parties? "Yes, the carpet matches the drapes." Oh. My. Gawd. Heat flooded my cheeks, and I ducked my head. "I can't believe I said that."

That tiny smile of hers never flickered, though. "Mine doesn't. Even when I have carpet."

"Shaving?" I couldn't believe I was having this conversation in the middle of a crowded bakery.

Bri shook her head. "Wax."

"Really? I tried that a couple of times and the pain…"

"Worth it to keep the stubble away."

If anyone was eavesdropping, it didn't show on their faces, and I doubted anyone cared. But it felt naughty to be talking about smooth, hair free nether regions with so many people around us. Like we were secretly sexy deviants.

Unfortunately, I couldn't figure out how to keep the tangent up. "That's not what you wanted to ask, though."

"It's a decent segue." Bri worked her jaw.

The fumble on her part was unexpected.

"I've heard rumors—not that everyone is talking about it, I promise, just a whisper here and there—that you and Scott have an open marriage?" Her voice grew soft at the end.

Ah. Familiar uncertainties and insecurity raced in, carried on every variation I'd heard of that question, and buoyed by half a dozen reactionary judgements. "It's not like we're out there sleeping with everyone. And there's nothing wrong with our marriage. It's really more of... I mean... He doesn't use it as an excuse to sleep around. He's never even been with someone else when I'm not there, and..." I caught my bottom lip between my teeth. This wasn't going well.

"You don't have to make excuses or apologize."

I shrugged. "It's habit."

"I get it. I only ask so I know, rather than assuming, before I keep flirting."

There was that jealousy again. She was out to break-fast with me, Scott wasn't even here, and she was asking about hitting on him? "Are you sure that's appropriate? He's your boss." That was meant to be concern, but all I heard was the cattiness in my own question.

The corners of her mouth tugged down. Only for a moment, but to me the slight frown was clear as day. "I meant with you."

Oh. *Oh.* "You were flirting with me?"

"Well, yeah. I get who Scott is. I see him almost every day, and going forward I'm going to look at him and be thinking *dude, your wife is so hot. How are you here and not at home?*"

The flush in my cheeks grew hotter at the way the compliment rolled easily off her lips. "We can't be screwing all the time—him and me."

"No. That wouldn't be practical." Her smile was

returning. "And honestly..." She furrowed her brow. "I was with a couple once, and it was bad. The sex was decent, but the fallout— Anyway, I'm interested in you. As long as he's not going to fire me over it." Bri slipped her hand across the table and nudged my fingertips with hers.

The touch was soft. Subtle. But it zinged through me like touching a live wire. "No. I can't promise a lot, but I can guarantee that." I'd been with Scott long enough, trusted him to the point where I could tell Bri this with confidence.

He was commanding, possessive, and cocky. But he knew how to temper it. Spite had never been on his list of traits, and he trusted me as much as I did him. "This has nothing to do with him, I give you my word. This is about two people who want to get to know each other better—you and me."

"Good." Bri's easy posture and expression slipped back in as she sipped her coffee. "Because I had this whole fantasy worked out in my head. you'd ask about my tattoos, and I'd tell you about a few. Ask if you'd ever considered your own."

"I could never do that." The idea of me getting some sort of permanent ink was far more terrifying than it was alluring. Though it did have an appeal. Maybe... "I couldn't."

"It's not proper, I get it. You said that in my head, too."

Bri had put thought into what might happen next between us. I couldn't help but be amused. It was also impossible to ignore that her fingers slipped closer, to cover mine. There was a low-grade hum under my skin that wanted more. Of her company. Of her touch.

"And I'd say, what if the marks weren't permanent?" Bri said. "I can give you some henna ones, to see how you like it."

"You could?"

"Absolutely."

I liked where this was going, so so much. "What happens next in this fantasy?"

"Doesn't matter." Her retort almost made me crash. "Because finding out what happens in real life will be way more fun than living it in my head over and over."

I liked this. "Can you really paint henna on me?"

"Do you want me to?"

"Yes." The word tumbled out so fast my tongue got twisted around the letters. "And you can tell me about your own ink when you do that?" She could tell me anything. Everything. I just had to learn about her.

Was I making a mistake? If I kept up this conversation, if I went down this path—wherever it lead—my life would never be the same.

That was both melodramatic and obvious. Every person I interacted with changed me.

But I couldn't shake the threads of worry that mingled with my excitement.

This was me being out of my comfort zone. Nothing more. "Let's go get supplies."

SIX
BRIENNE

ONE OF THE MOST IMPORTANT LESSONS I LEARNED FROM my father was that nothing was forever, especially not relationships. That meant enjoying the fun moments when they came along was key.

Kenzie was fun. So far, lots of fun. A little awkward, a little naive for someone older than me, and a lot reserved. But still fun.

I wasn't looking to be part of her life long term. Today would be sufficient as long as it continued to be enjoyable.

We hit up a tea shop a few doors down from the bakery that also had henna.

"I didn't even know this was here," Kenzie looked around the small place in awe as we walked through the front door.

"Hardly anyone does." The store was tucked between an art gallery and an alley, and most people thought the entrance was just a side door to someplace else. "But it's been here for decades. Sometimes I think it

42

might be owned by a god, trying to hide his identity from the world."

"Can I help you?" A chipper young woman stepped in our path, shattering the calm in the room and startling us both.

Kenzie laughed nervously. That was pretty adorable. I wanted to know more about her. Push her limits a hint. See what it was like to slide my fingers inside her. To taste her and make her come.

I told the girl what we were looking for, and a moment later she was ringing us up.

Kenzie called for a ride to my car. We didn't talk much on the trip back to the lodge where I was parked. I suspected she wasn't interested in saying many things in front of a stranger.

To me, most of the world was strangers. I preferred it that way. Connections rarely lasted, and when they snapped—

The great thing about dating half a couple, especially a couple as much in love as Scott and Kenzie, was it helped guarantee she wouldn't want long term from me. I didn't think Scott would be an issue. He was friendly with everyone, I wasn't getting any special treatment, and if Kenzie didn't think he would fire me, that was all I needed to know.

On the other hand, Kenzie's insecurities would keep her from getting attached.

No one would get hurt. Not the way my father hurt me. Not the way the last couple hurt me when they treated me like a doll then threw me out. Not the way

43

people got hurt when one got closer than the other, then the other walked away.

Nope. There would be none of that here.

When we reached my trusty, rusty old Subaru, I drove us back to Kenzie and Scott's place. My station wagon looked out of place in their sweeping driveway, but the car got me from place to place and that was all I needed it to do.

Inside, I set us up in the kitchen, on tile, near the sink. "Where do you want it?" I asked.

"Where should I put it?" Kenzie countered.

Inside of her thigh could be fun. Playful. Maybe a bit too tempting though. "Shoulder blade?"

"Perfect." Kenzie grinned. "But then I need something to cover up, don't I?"

Not really. I could paint her while she was topless. If she was asking, I would comply. I looked around the room, and my sight landed on an apron. "How about that?"

She nodded. "Give me a second." She grabbed the apron, stepped from the room, and returned a moment later with her top and bra gone, and the apron in place. The way the fabric hung showed off the perfect amount of sideboob and smooth, pale skin.

Yummy.

"Have a seat." I gestured to the chair. With a little more prep, I started in, painting thin, flowing lines along her skin.

"Where did you learn this?" Kenzie asked as I worked.

It was actually one of my better memories. My one

long-term connection besides Grandpa. "My best friend, Manda, does this at Ren Faires, parties, conventions, things like that. She taught me when I left home, so for a few years."

"That sounds like fun," Kenzie said.

The conversation faded again as I focused. Every time I ran my fingers over her skin, with each soft sigh she made when the brush met her shoulder or back, want pulsed inside me. More than once, I caught myself fighting the desire to lean in and draw my lips along her neck. The long, slender curve was made more tempting by the way we'd pulled her hair into a messy bun, to keep the blond strands from getting in the way.

"All done." I put down my supplies and stepped back, ignoring the disappointment that slammed into me at not having an excuse to touch her anymore. I shifted my attention instead to the simple trio of flowers I'd painted onto her. They were intertwined with a lace-like pattern, and the entire thing was a stunning contrast to her pale skin. "Do you want to see?"

"Of course." Kenzie was on her feet in an instant. She reached for my hand then dropped her arm. "The master bath has the best mirrors."

I followed her across the living room, to the doors on the other side of the house. The bedroom was decorated like the rest of the house—beiges and off whites that reflected nothing of Kenzie or Scott. I suspected a place like this was more for guests and business contacts than for them.

The view of the mountains was stunning, though.

The bathroom was bigger than the bedroom in my

apartment. A free standing tub big enough for two people stood by another huge window, and across from that were two sinks and a bank of mirrors that covered an entire wall.

This was a sharp reminder that these people lived a lifestyle similar to the one I'd escaped hit me hard, and I wasn't sure why. I'd spent the night, the last few hours, in a large home at the edge of one of the richest cities in the state. Why was I surprised to see that reflected around me?

I shook the discomfort aside. "Do you have a hand-held mirror?"

Kenzie opened one of the half dozen drawers for the item. I positioned her with her back to the mirror, swept her hair away from the new lines, and let her take a look. I didn't realize I was stroking my fingers along the nape of her neck, until she sighed softly.

The sound and the shivers it sent spilling through me were both signs I should pull away. It was one thing to mention fantasy and flirting in conversation, but making it physical...

Who was I kidding? I'd already made up my mind. I continued to trail my fingers along her shoulder, around the new art, and down her spine. The tiny sounds she made with each touch were musical temptation.

"What's it like?" Kenzie asked. "Being at an orgy, I mean. Not the generic answer you gave me before. What's it *like*?"

Well, fuck. It would be rude not to answer the woman. "In some ways, it's like any sex. How good or bad it is depends on the people you're with and if you click."

Kenzie licked her bottom lip. "What about in other ways?"

"There's a freedom in it. As long as you can find a willing partner, you can try most anything you want. But you also don't have to try anything. You're in an entire room full of people fucking, but no one is going to pressure you into it if you say *no*."

"So if I approached you…" Her voice had gone so soft I had to strain to hear. "Would you explore with me? In front of all those people?"

"Yes." I took the smaller mirror from her and set it on the counter, before turning her to face me. I tucked her hair behind her ear. She had such pretty blue eyes. Such a kissable shine on her lips. Such a sweet, sincere expression. And it'd been ages since I'd clicked so well with someone. "It seems like a shame to wait for an orgy though, when we're already here."

"I like the way you think." Kenzie tilted her head up and pressed her lips to mine. She pulled away so quickly, the kiss was sinfully chaste.

I wanted more than a little peck on the lips. A lot more. I pressed into her with a hungry kiss, lingering on the way she gasped and tasted and felt. She was softness with the spiciest hint of defiance, and I was going to take everything she let me sample.

"Tell me what you like." I dragged my mouth down her neck, and tugged the tie free on her apron to let it tumble to the floor. Her whimper was its own reward, though the way she stripped off my shirt, was pretty good too.

"Most of what I've done before now hasn't been deliberate so much as stumbled on. With another woman I mean," she said.

I drew one of her nipples into my mouth and sucked and nibbled. It was easy to start with what I liked, and go from there, and it was intoxicating to hear her reactions and at the same time imagine being in her place. I focused on one breast until she was squirming, then moved to the other side. "But you know what you enjoy."

"I'm more interested in what I like that I don't know about." Kenzie tugged playfully at my bottoms.

I liked the sound of that. Exploration was always fun. Diving into tasting her. Enjoying her hand gliding under my yoga pants and over my panties. Pushing her leggings to the ground, to tease her through the thin patch of cotton covering her pussy.

It was tempting to stay like this, letting our hands roam each other's bodies and figuring out what buttons did what as I touched each new part of her.

But this wasn't that kind of relationship. This was fucking. "Tell me a fantasy no one knows," I said.

Kenzie's breath hitched. "I don't…"

"You do. You have at least one you haven't even shared with Scott." I wouldn't keep his name out of the bedroom or pretend he didn't exist.

"Maybe." Her voice was playful again.

"Does it have to do with orgies?"

"Probably."

Nice. I scraped my teeth over her skin and sucked along her neck, while I teased insistent fingers over the damp barrier keeping me from entering her. "Tell me."

"I want to be taken—used—in front of a crowd, by another woman."

Not super detailed, but still hot. I leaned into the kissing and physical coaxing, hoping for more.

"Not degraded," Kenzie said between gasps. "I don't want to be spit on or called a whore—not that I have a problem with it, I just don't think it's for me —but…"

The trailing off was both alluring and frustrating. Desire climbed inside me. I wanted to feel more of her. Taste all of her. Have her mouth on more of me and do the same to her. "You can tell me." I made the words softer but more commanding. "About how you want to be seen for you. You don't want to have to hide anything. You want that room full of people to look at you and know who the fuck *you* are, and that they can't have you. Only I can."

I didn't mean to add that last bit.

"Exactly," Kenzie said breathlessly.

"And?"

"How do you know there's an *and*?"

I teased under the elastic on her thigh, brushing the edge of her mound with my finger. "Lucky guess."

"I want it to be just a little wrong. Just a hint of dirty."

Dirtier than being fucked in front of a room full of people who couldn't touch us. I liked it. I yanked her panties to her knees in a single swift tug, exposing her ass, and grabbed her hairbrush from the counter. I smacked her ass with the bristles.

Kenzie's surprised yelp ended in a sigh.

Oh, God. I was making myself wet too. "Do you like that?"

She bit her bottom lip. "I don't know. I think you have to do it again so I can figure it out."

Too, too fun. I alternated smacking one of her ass cheeks and then the other, making sure to keep the strikes light. It didn't take long before her behind was bright red and she was moaning. "Just a little wrong?" I repeated her earlier words.

"Just a smidge."

Just a hint of dirty. I switched my grip on the brush, slid the end along her slit, and slipped the handle inside her.

She gasped and squirmed and pressed into the makeshift dildo. I fucked her with the hairbrush, enjoying the way she rocked against it. Devouring her moans as they grew louder. More punctuated.

"Don't let it fall out." I warned and pulled my hand away. The brush stayed in place as turned her to face me and coaxed her to her knees.

She looked up at me, eyes wide and cheeks flushed.

I tangled my fingers in her hair. "Imagine an audience full of people who want you. People who have told you your entire life that you have to be what they say." Was I talking to her or myself? "People who have no idea who you are or what you really want. Tell them all to go fuck themselves."

Kenzie's smile was the most delicious combination

of sweet and wicked, and she pulled my panties down. She dragged her tongue along my pussy and my strangled groan escaped at that next hint of pleasure.

I gripped her long, blond strands tightly in my fist, guiding her as she licked inside me. Up to my clit. Back down again. When she wrapped her mouth around my clit and sucked, release surged forward in a surprising burst.

Something clattered—a hairbrush hitting tile—but I didn't care. This felt good. Better than good. This was incredible. Kenzie sucked on me until I was writhing against her face and my legs wobbled.

This really was that perfect blend of fun and dirty.

I pulled her to her feet, using the counter to keep me on mine, and claimed her mouth in a hungry kiss. The way our mouths crushed together was sloppy and wet and desperate.

And I wanted to make her come.

Not here. We needed comfort. I tangled my fingers with hers and led her to the guest room. "On the bed," I ordered.

She complied.

Kenzie looked so stunning, stretched out, naked, and flushed with desire. If this was the only time we were going to do this, I wanted her to remember it. *I* wanted to remember it.

I worshiped her body with my mouth, kissing her breasts, sucking on her neck, and devouring her pussy until she screamed and screamed again.

Time fell away. Nothing else existed until she shuddered from my hungry mouth, and gave a light laugh as she asked me to stop.

I climbed up her body for more soft kisses, and to wrap my body around hers.

"Can I keep you the rest of the weekend?" Kenzie asked softly.

Keep. The word pinged against my brain like a hammer, and I fumbled for an answer.

"I don't like sleeping alone." Kenzie seemed to be responding to my silence.

Once upon a time, being used as a bed warmer would've bothered me. I was fine with it these days. It meant no attachment. Once Kenzie had her man back, she'd be done with me, we'd both have had our fun, and life would go back to normal. As in, I would occasionally see Kenzie in the halls at work, and that was it.

Until then, I liked her company, and I was having fun.

"Sure. I'm all yours, but only for the weekend."

"Perfect." Kenzie snuggled closer.

SEVEN

SCOTT

I BOTH LOATHED AND LOVED THE PERSON WHO INVENTED red eye flights. Brilliant way to get from one coast to the other when most people were sleeping. But after spending all weekend in the Nashville offices, cooped up but diving into some intensely incredible brainstorming, I was both too tired and too wired to do any of that same sleeping myself.

The light from my laptop screen was the brightest thing in the cabin, because trying to check items off my to-do list was better than staring at the inside of my eyelids, wishing for a few minutes of unconsciousness. Except a long screen full of legalese stared back at me, reminding me I had trouble comprehending these details when I was fully awake.

Why couldn't I decide if I wanted to write this stupid memoir?

Agreeing to consider a contract seemed like a good idea at the time, but putting my stories down on paper was a different beast than telling them off-the-cuff-at-parties. Could I translate one medium to the other?

Plus, I'd been there, done that as far as my past was concerned. I'd rather be doing more of what I'd just done in Nashville—diving into brand new ideas and solutions—than lingering in memories. Nothing was more incredible than coming up with new ideas and bringing them to life. Perfecting them.

I was jarred from a barely-sleep by the plane taxiing to our gate, and the flight attendant telling us it was five-forty-five local time.

Fortunately, I didn't check any bags, so less than half an hour later I had texted Kenzie *I'm home*, and was on the road and heading for our condo downtown.

When I walked in the front door, the smell of fresh coffee pushed away some of the cobwebs in my mind, and seeing her in the kitchen in nothing but one of my old shirts helped wake me up further.

"How was your flight? Do you have time to sleep this morning?" She asked.

After more than five years of coming home to her, I still believed Kenzie was the best thing to ever happen to me. I grabbed a mug and poured myself some coffee. "It was a flight. And no. Meetings all day." I drained half my cup in a single swallow, not caring that the dark liquid scalded as it went down.

Her pout was exaggerated. "I guess I'm going back to bed alone. Again."

"Uh-huh." I brushed my lips over hers. I was certain of two things—she was up before I landed, and she hadn't spent most of her weekend alone. "Give me the sordid details of what happened in the mountains when I get back tonight?"

Kenzie leaned deeper into the kiss, teasing her tongue over my bottom lip.

That was fun and new. I slid my hand to the back of her neck to capture her.

She pulled away with a playful smirk. "My sex life doesn't exist to be your spank bank material." Her tone was light and teasing.

Bri must've been a lot of fun. I was glad, but the sneaking jealousy that joined the feeling was also new. Different. I didn't care for it. "I wish I could stay here today."

Kenzie tugged me closer again and rested her cheek against my chest. "I'll miss you."

It was easy to linger, frozen in this pose. To feel her familiar warmth course through me. Dwell on that connection. I didn't want to summon the willpower to pull away, but I did it anyway and kissed her on the top of the head. "I have to get ready."

"I know." She straightened in her seat.

I rushed through a shower and getting dressed. I'd be dragging by noon, but for now I could face the world. Before I left, I stole another long kiss from Kenzie, then I headed to the office.

I was passing the cafeteria when I caught voices drifting from one of the tables. Something about clothing and skin textures.

I couldn't pass up a good tech conversation, especially about my game, so I followed the sound to its source.

Elliot and Judith were two of my Vice Presidents, and had been with the company through being bought out, pushed out, name changes, staff changes…

There were few people I trusted more. Kenzie. My business partner, Zach. His wife Rae. Those were top tier. Then Elliot, Judith, and my other VP, Chloe.

"Hey." I made my bark intentionally rough, and Elliot and Judith jumped. "You know the rules—no hallway meetings."

Elliot snorted. "The what?"

"I don't think that word means what you think it means," Judith said.

Smart asses. "What word? Rules? Pretty sure I used it correctly."

"The fact that you're not positive proves my point." Judith sipped her coffee, not trying to hide the smugness that implied she thought she'd won.

She hadn't, but I wanted to go back to what they were talking about before I interrupted. "Clothing. Skin. Fill me in."

"We're figuring out the next step for conquering the world," Judith said.

Uh-huh.

"That's what she's doing. I just want more sex in my games." Elliot's answer sounded far more plausible.

Also, an easy opening. If they could give me shit about *rules*… "Not getting enough at home?"

Elliot's pout was exaggerated and ridiculous. "My waifu pillow stopped putting out. Something about me working too much?"

"Sounds like a personal problem to me," I teased.

These weren't the kind of jokes I'd make with most people; even I had my limits, but I'd known Judith for years and Elliot even longer. It would be unnatural to *not* tease them.

Judith raised her brows. "Which part is his problem? The long hours or that he thinks he's married to a body pillow?"

"Don't you talk about Kimiko like that." Elliot smacked his palms on the table.

Judith and I laughed.

This was what I needed this morning, since I couldn't stay home with Kenzie. The weekend of problem solving was great, but these were my people. My friends. "Give me a straight answer." They both snorted, and I rolled my eyes. "I heard something about the clothing and skin modules. Fill me in." Before I started to sound like a broken record.

"Elliot was serious. How do we put more sex into the *X* franchise?" Judith said.

I hated questions like this. Not because it was a bad idea, but because it was a reminder there were some things we couldn't do now that we were so big. Saying *we don't* was the worst answer I could think of. "You make a new game." As the words rolled off my tongue, my mind perked up, but I couldn't grasp why.

Judith frowned.

"Kimiko wouldn't go for that." Elliot ran with the waifu pillow gag. "It means even more time in the office."

"Yeah." I wasn't all here, though. This conversation was important. I needed to follow—

"I have to get upstairs." Judith stood. "Walk me to the elevator, Scott?"

Interesting. What did she want to talk about?

"No telling secrets about me." Elliot shouted at our backs as we walked away.

"He already knows about your funny looking dong." Judith hollered back.

Ludicrous. Fantastic. "Actually, I didn't. I don't need to hear that shit."

Judith shrugged. "You wanted to be part of the conversation. But fine, moving on. Have you seen the news?"

I raised an eyebrow.

"No then."

I didn't need to answer her question, she already knew what I'd say. Industry news was ninety percent gossip, most of it recycled, and I stayed away from it when I was engrossed in important things.

"What did I miss?" I asked. It was something important if she was bringing it up.

"Friday's party made headlines."

One of the things I appreciated about Judith was her gift for succinctness. However, now that we'd moved away from teasing she was being too concise.

"The investor party always makes headlines," I said. It was one of the things we were known for. People would be scanning every piece of information we shared, looking for a hint of what was coming next.

There was nothing worth talking about this year. Same shit, same core game, different wrapping paper.

The thought made me realize I hated how predictable we'd become, but I shoved the reaction aside. "Give me the highlights about what they think is a big deal."

"They're talking about how Chester Walker Sr. sent his granddaughter in his place instead of sending Chester Jr. What could it possibly mean for the future of gaming?"

They were talking about Bri. There was nothing to say, but the news didn't sit well with me, and I needed to discard some of my sleep-deprivation to figure out why not. "She was just another guest."

The elevator doors slid open, and we stepped on.

"Another guest you and Kenzie spent most of the night talking to. The woman who's been working here for more than two years without telling anyone who she's related to. Whose father—"

"Thinks I'm his biggest rival. Yeah, I get it." Or rather, I personally thought the assumption was stupid. But if the rest of the industry assumed it was impossible for three people to have a conversation without it being a conspiracy, "I'll deal with it."

The elevator stopped on the floor for Innovation—Judith's specialty. "Did you know?" She held the Door Closed button, locking us in place.

Know...? "That Brienne was Chester's daughter?" I'd known when Chloe hired her. So much for continuing to keep it a secret. "Does it matter?" Of course it did, or the three of us wouldn't have hidden it. Because Brienne was here based on her own skills. Her job had nothing to do with her father.

"You have a plan. I'm going to trust that." Judith let the doors slide open.

"Thanks." I didn't have a plan at all, but I appreciated the vote of confidence. Especially from her. Judith was plans within plans and all of them sprinkled with every imaginable detail.

I couldn't do that, but I respected her for it.

Judith headed to her office, and I rode the elevator the rest of the way up.

There was a fine line to walk with news like this. Without reading a single article, I could assume people were talking about the fact that we'd kept Bri's employment a secret.

Ridiculous concept, since we didn't make the pasts of any new employees public—who the fuck cared that our newest artist used to be a boudoir photographer or that we had a QA guy who grew up in the circus?

Gossip pages didn't care about the individual.

At my desk, I worked my way through the emails that needed my attention, and clicked through to the news. Most of the articles were little more than cut and paste versions of one another. Some people managed to come up with different speculations—Rinslet was buying out Chester Jr. He was buying out us. Regardless, Bri was supposedly negotiating on his behalf.

As if.

I could guess how she felt about her father and his business based on the fact she didn't have access to his money, and she worked hard to make sure no one knew she was related. I hoped this wasn't too hard on her, for this all to be coming out now

It was in the last dredges of the articles that one caught my eye. The site was familiar to me, but the article writer wasn't. They were speculating that based on my past, based on Bri's, something more than business was going on.

What past? He asked. *Don't tell me you've never heard of the Cord orgy days. Rumor is Ms. Walker has similar skeletons in her closet.*

Fuck. Someone had to dredge up the past. Of course.

I didn't care what they said about me—the list had gotten long over the years, and this didn't come close to some of the worst theories that floated around.

But if this fucked with Kenzie, if it came back on Bri, I'd be furious. Which meant I needed to act now, before things got out of hand.

EIGHT
BRIENNE

THIS WEEKEND WAS INCREDIBLE. *KENZIE* WAS INCREDIBLE. When I dropped her off at her condo in town Sunday night, I'd refused to let us make any specific plans. *We'll run into each other again* seemed smartest.

But Monday as I got ready for work, I was still thinking about her. Not the sex—though *yummy*—but the conversations.

I could enjoy the buzz a little longer, as long as I remembered this was all memories. Not a promise of future fun. This didn't mean anything beyond what had already happened.

My phone rang as I was finishing up my make-up, and a picture of me and my best friend Manda grinned up at me.

What was I going to tell her? I had no idea, beyond *Oh. My. God. I had a blast with the boss's wife, what do I do?*

I hit *Speaker* and left the phone on the counter as I put the final touches on my eyeliner. "Hey, bitch."

"Don't you *bitch* me. You haven't earned that."

Manda's tone was teasing, but something lay underneath.

"What did I do?"

"Only made me hear gossip *about you* from Jenquiry's Morning Kick in the Pants, rather than telling me yourself. You couldn't spare ten minutes between Friday and now to call me?"

What the...? "There's no gossip." And I'd thought about calling her last night, but I wanted to linger in the glow, keep the warm fuzzy Kenzie feeling to myself, just a little longer.

"The rest of the world disagrees. At least the rest of your world."

People didn't know, did they? Sure we went to breakfast together. And dinner. Two women—friends—hanging out.

"What gossip, Manda?" I pushed.

She sighed. "That you had dinner with Scott McAllister Friday night."

"I went to an investor dinner. Along with a billion other people."

"And now the world knows you work for him, and you also spent all that time talking to him."

No. "That's not... I didn't... I swear to you Manda. That is not what happened. I'm not hiding anything from you." Well, one thing, but until I had more details, I was holding onto my story. "Jenquiry, you said?"

The Jenquiry was a vlogger who covered game industry news. Scott and Rinslet were featured on a regular basis—sometimes praised and others roasted—but I was no one in that industry, and Jen wasn't a gossip columnist. Well, maybe of industry speculation, but not personal lives.

"Yeah. Check her out. Call me back if you need anything."

That didn't sound ominous at all. "I will." I hung up. Makeup would have to be done for the morning. Seconds later I was pulling up the video in question, titled *Darth Walker Seduces the Light. Rinslet, I am your father.*

Scott and Rinslet were known for being random and irreverent, but also overall had a reputation as a great company to work for, who made games most people liked to play. The worst thing they'd been accused of recently was *Virtue Signaling.*

Whatever.

On the other hand, Chester Walker Jr. was known as the creeping darkness. He bought out smaller companies. He ruined people's favorite indie games. Yeah, my dad was Emperor Palpatine.

I watched Jen's video with a sick horror churning in my gut. She was focused on several stills and short videos of me talking with Scott and Kenzie at the dinner. She broke down the better known games Dad had destroyed when he absorbed the developers. And she focused heavily on the fact that his estranged daughter was chatting happily with his biggest rival.

I doubted Scott saw things that way, but to Dad, Rinslet was the one company he'd love to sink his fingers into. To get a hold of their titles. Their talent. To take them off the map so quickly that literally nuking them would be less effective.

Was everyone talking about this? A quick scan of

industry news, and even a couple of brief stories from national outlets, showed that yes—the world thought I was acting on Dad's behalf, to get him and Scott talking.

Fuck. I wanted to throw my phone or scream or do *something* to tell these idiots they were reading the situation wrong. *I'm not negotiating on my father's behalf, I just want to sleep with my boss's wife. Again..*

It was time to put *that* aspect of things out of my mind.

And if I posted a note on social media saying this was all a big misunderstanding, would anyone even listen?

My phone rang again, startling me, and this time *Daddy Dearest* flashed on the screen.

I'd heard from him once in the last year, and it was a week ago when he realized where I would be spending last weekend. It was no coincidence he was calling now, and he was the last person I wanted to talk to.

As his call went to voicemail, a text came through. *You know Scott McAllister.*

Fuck you, old man. I deleted the message without responding.

I spent the drive to the office pushing the bad press to the back of my mind, in hopes I'd be able to get work done today. In a day or two, Digital Media would do something to piss off the gaming world, and when they did people would forget I existed, let alone who I was related to or where I worked.

Then I could tell Manda what happened with Kenzie, she could swoon with me, and we could go get drunk and figure out who we wanted to go home with next.

When I got to the office, every hallway I walked down, every room I passed, went quiet when they saw me. People who were normally friendly glanced sideways at me or ignored me completely.

By the time I settled at my desk, my brain was a wreck. How was I going to get anything done?

I was trying anyway, sifting through Chloe's calendar for the day and catching up on emails, when she arrived.

She paused in front of my desk, the first person to look me in the eye this morning, and gave me a sympathetic smile. "I know you didn't want this to get out. I'm sorry. How are you holding up?" She asked.

"I'll be okay." Saying the words out loud didn't make them any easier to believe. "I'll lose myself in work and this will all pass before I know it." Nothing about my tone was convincing.

"I'm sure it will go exactly like that." If Chloe was trying to reassure me, it didn't work. "Let me know what I can do."

I nodded. "Thanks."

Industry news, the tendency of people to gossip and speculate about *everything* had cost her boyfriend his job here. They'd recovered, differently than I'm sure either of them expected, but if they could do it, I could do the same.

The longer I worked, the more I was able to immerse myself in day-to-day tasks. This wouldn't be a big deal. I'd keep reminding the world that I was estranged from my father, they'd go back to ignoring me, and life would return to normal.

A few hours in, Scott called my desk phone.

"Good morning." I employed the same polite, generic tone I always used with the executives.

"I need five minutes of your time."

Mine? Not Chloe's? "Now?" Not my best response, but a margin better than if I'd asked *why*?

"Now." There was only command in his voice.

Talking to him was better than talking to my father or listening to whispers when I did things like walked into a meeting with Chloe, to take notes for her.

What did he want to talk about? Besides the obvious. Would this be a *stay away from my wife* conversation? Probably not a *we should make this a threesome*, however, while he didn't seem like that kind of creep, sometimes my radar broke when I met a gorgeous, fun woman who was already in a relationship.

Speculation was easy, but not nearly as effective as talking. "I'm on my way."

As I strode toward his office, his assistant wasn't as his desk, and Scott's door was open. Neither was unusual.

"Come on in," he said as I crossed the threshold. "Close the door and have a seat." He pointed at the chair across from him.

I swallowed, trying to work some moisture into my dry throat, and did as requested. As commanded? There was no room in his tone for argument.

Scott tilted his head to the side and studied me with a furrowed brow. "I'm making you nervous."

Was this what he was like in the bedroom? All command and easy confidence?

What the fuck, brain?

"Yes." Lying wouldn't serve any purpose.

"That's not my intent." Scott's voice softened. "It's about this morning's news. Nothing more."

I could've guessed that, but I appreciated the qualifier. "Okay."

One corner of his mouth pulled up. "You're familiar with our company's fraternization policies."

What did that have to do with either subject? "Yes." Short version was, we didn't have many. They seemed to be in place for legal reasons, and were all worded around people turning down unwanted advances without their jobs being at risk. There was little verbiage around employees dating each other.

Did he mean his question to be reassuring, because it wasn't.

"Good," Scott said. "And you're aware that your father and I have a history."

Could people please stop talking about my father and let me get back to my life? "I am. But that's all between you and him. I'm not on his side. In anything. I wasn't trying—"

"I can make the headlines from today go away quickly."

I was so confused. Was there a structure to his half of the conversation or was he saying random things to keep me on my toes? "What will it cost me?"

Stop seeing my wife.

Let's have a threesome.

You can't work here anymore.

The last one terrified me. I loved this job.

"It won't cost you anything." For the first time this morning, Scott's smooth tone wavered. "I want to make sure you're okay with what I'm going to do. Chloe would never forgive me if we lost you—you're one of our best. But dealing in favors is dangerous. This isn't tit for tat."

"What's your plan?" I couldn't keep guessing what was on his mind.

"Make an official statement. Something simple. Your father has wanted my ear for years, and I found out his daughter worked for me. Friday night's conversation was me making sure you and I didn't have an issue, and Kenzie was there to ensure you were comfortable with the conversation."

Oh. Basic. Simple. "And that's it?"

"Yes."

It wouldn't magically make things disappear, but it would mean a lot of people would get bored quickly and move on. "That's straightforward and drama free." I shouldn't be surprised, but this company usually played up their headlines. Rode them for any publicity they could get.

"This isn't something that needs to be fed," Scott said. "Any questions?"

"Who are you?" Oops. Not what I meant to ask. It was too late to take it back, though. Not that I would if I could.

His stoic mask slipped again. This time for longer. Amusement reached his eyes. His serious, business-like attitude returned quickly. "I'm sure I don't understand."

"I'm sure." *Why are you acting like this? What did you do with the real Scott McAllister? Where's the man who approached me Friday night? Is he locked in that big filing cabinet behind you?*

He huffed a sigh. "If this was just about you and me having dinner, if it didn't touch anyone else, I wouldn't give a fuck. I wish I could ignore this until people got bored with it. I'd love for that to be an option. It won't work that way. This is the next best step."

"Putting on a mask and pretending you're one of them?" I should stop now. Why was I needling him over a reasonable answer?

Scott twisted his mouth and stared at me. "From the woman who dressed perfectly to the crowd on Friday night, and hid in the back corner, not speaking unless spoken to."

Because I was there in my grandfather's place. Because I wasn't representing myself. Because—"Point taken."

"Since we're dropping the bullshit..." Scott leaned in, his fingers interlaced and his hands resting on his desk. "What Kenzie does is about Kenzie. She and I don't keep secrets, but she's her own person. Period."

Was that permission? Acceptance? It sounded like both. "Thank you. For letting me know, I mean."

"Go back to work. You have important things to do." Scott waved his fingers.

Apparently that was that.

So why did I feel like I was waiting for the other shoe to drop as I headed back to my desk?

I settled in again, and when my cell phone rang, I grabbed it without thinking. "Yellow."

"I was starting to think you were screening my calls." My father's voice was like claws raking over my skin, and my nausea surged in.

It was tempting to hang up, but that wouldn't stop him from calling back. This conversation needed to happen, if for no other reason than it gave me a chance to tell him to leave me alone. "And yet that didn't keep you from calling again. And again. And again."

"So you were screening me." There was no warmth in his voice, but he hadn't insulted me yet—either directly or otherwise—so he must be up to something.

"What can I do for you?"

"Get me a meeting with Scott McAllister."

"No." I could've said *that's not up to me*, but I liked being able to hold this little bit of power over my father.

The sigh he made was one I'd heard countless times in my life. It was that *I'm so disappointed in you* sound that used to make my insides curdle and tears prick my eyelids.

Now it was just background noise.

"I have an opportunity to help push this new rendering engine of his at SXSW," my dad said.

I couldn't hide my bark of amusement. Was he serious? I may not know most of the more technical terminology, but I'd been in enough meetings over the past several months to realize what he said had nothing to do with what we were working on in Nashville. "Uh-huh. *Rendering engine.* Try again."

"Your grandfather is being moved into hospice." His

71

news took a right turn that sent me toppling off my tracks.

Wait. What? Ice sank in my gut like a stone. "You didn't lead with that? You didn't put that in any of your messages?"

"It's news best delivered during a conversation." Now the edge was creeping into his voice. That hint of disdain that lingered whenever we spoke.

A few years ago, Grandpa had been moved into a nursing home, and my dad had left explicit instructions with staff to not let me talk to him. I'd managed a few calls and an in-person visit, but after this last one, where Grandpa shocked the fuck out of me by asking me to attend the Rinslet investor party in his place, he implied future conversations were going to be more difficult to arrange.

Did Grandpa know that his health was on this kind of decline? The fact that he may have, that he'd hidden it from me, made my gut churn. Why hadn't I noticed? Heard something in his voice? Anything.

"I'd like to see him," I said.

"That won't be possible. I'll let you know when he passes, and keep you up to date on memorial arrangements." He disconnected before I could ask more.

Now I was sick. I swallowed the bile back, but grief bubbled inside at the thought of not being able to say *goodbye* to Grandpa.

NINE
KENZIE

IF I LOOKED BACK ON MY LIFE TEN YEARS AGO, OR EVEN six or seven, my days were filled with a nine to five grind, obliterating a number of personal time boundaries in favor of getting the job done. Of proving I was the right person for whatever that job was.

In contrast, spending my days keeping a loose eye on the cleaning staff and my nights making sure my husband slept should be heaven.

Gawd I was bored.

I don't remember last week feeling like this. Or the week before. This week my mind had enough free space to daydream about Bri every time I paused for a moment or two.

And I paused for a lot of moments. Surely this wasn't all I did with my time.

By Thursday I was counting the minutes to the lunch plans I had with a friend. I needed something to keep me from spending the entire afternoon on the couch, replaying the weekend I'd had with Bri—the fun parts and the naughty parts. But especially the naughtily fun parts.

I arrived at lunch early, but that wasn't new for me, and Barb was five minutes late. That was fine. I'd spent my twenties working with corporate jackasses who believed the world ran on their clock. At least she was profusely sorry when she arrived.

We grabbed coffees and pastries from the cafe inside The Grand America, and took seats in a cozy corner at the back of the dining room. We exchanged polite, generic versions of *how are you?* When she asked if I'd done anything fun this weekend after the dinner, I almost said *this fun woman with some gorgeous tattoos gave me the most incredible orgasm with her mouth, and what led up to it was so dirty.*

It was a shame responses like that were frowned upon when planning charity dinners with the wives of some of the wealthiest men in town.

Wait. It was a shame? I didn't talk about things like that. Who was I?

As she dove into the conversation, I found myself comparing my outfit to hers. I'd worn a pastel blouse. Simple but expensive jewelry. Makeup that was meant to be noticed but still look natural.

She looked about the same, so why did I feel like I clashed with her today? Her hair was perfectly smooth. Not a strand out of place. Mine had refused to stay in a neat bun and hung in boring strands around my face.

I hadn't dealt with insecurities like this for years. They'd faded into almost nothing the longer I spent with Scott, so why were they back now?

What would Bri do?

I knew what Scott would do. When I first met him, one of the first times we'd gone to lunch, I took him to a nicer steakhouse to *teach him how to behave.*

Uh-huh.

He'd shown up in torn jeans and a faded T-shirt. But he'd also known almost the entire staff already, and was friendly to all of them.

Would he do the same today if he were meeting us here?

He'd probably joke *I'm only here for Kenzie.*

How many times had I heard him say that recently?

"Is now a bad time?" Barb's question jarred me from my rambling thoughts.

I shook the wandering aside. "No, this is perfect. I'm sorry."

"Are you sure you didn't get up to anything fun this weekend?" She teased.

I really, really did. "Nothing worth mentioning. Where were we? I promise I'm paying attention."

"I was saying while we're here, we should check out their venue. It might be a great place for us to do this. Imagine their main hall, the chandeliers, satin table-cloths, caviar, and sashimi tuna. That chef who's big right now on the cooking channel..." She painted an extravagant picture.

"It sounds incredible."

"Then what's wrong?" Barb asked.

What was...? Crap, I was frowning. "I just... it all sounds like so much." Because now I was remembering the conversation with Bri and Scott, about the Konsoles for Kids auction and how part of its beauty was its simplicity.

Barb's expression made me think I was speaking a foreign language. She gave a brief shake of her head. "With your skills, most of it will be donated. And it's for such a great cause."

True. We were fundraising for a group of shelters that helped people escape abusive home lives.

And if I made my calls, got those donations sent directly to the shelters instead, those people—mostly women and children—would probably eat better than they had... possibly ever.

But it wouldn't be a long-term solution, and a charity event like this rallied people. It drew them to support whatever name they were asked to write on their checks.

"Kenzie?"

I shook the thoughts aside. "Yeah, I can totally do that. Let's go take a look at the venue while we're here. Like you said."

I managed to act more like my polite, personable self for the rest of the afternoon as we checked out the ballroom at The Grand America and then toured a couple of other nearby places.

Why was my brain so out of sorts today? I needed to do something about my attitude before I met with Barb again.

Just as I was pulling into the parking garage at home, Scott called.

"Hey, brainy boy." I lingered in the driver's seat as my tension slipped away.

"Hey, pretty lady." His voice sent happy tingles racing over me. Always. "Up to anything interesting?"

"Sitting in the garage. Playing with myself." Who said that? Me? No.

Scott sucked in a sharp breath, and I swore I could feel his reaction over the lines. "In that case, I hope all the wrong people see." His voice dropped an octave.

I wanted to play. To have fun. I was also distinctly aware of my surroundings, and this wasn't me. "What's up?"

Was that a pause? "I have to head to Nashville again tonight." He shifted topics faster and more seamlessly than my sister changing TV channels when she was bored. "I tried to fix it remotely, but they need me on site."

Oh. I tucked aside my disappointment at another solo night of sleeping. "I can pack you a bag and drop it off. Say *hi*." Say *bye*. Because if I waited for him to come home, I'd see him for about two minutes, and this way I could steal more of his time.

"And if you come here, you can see Bri," Scott teased.

Heat flooded my face. "No. Maybe. But no."

"Uh-huh. I have another meeting. I'll see you when you get here?"

"Yup. Love you."

"Love you too, gorgeous."

I hung up as Scott did, headed upstairs to pack a bag for him, and was heading to the Rinslet building a short while later. I pulled in as people were leaving for the day, which left some great spots near the elevator for me to snag. After I climbed from my car, I paused. Would I be more likely to find Scott in his office?

I sent him a quick text. *Downstairs. Should I come up, or…?*

"Or what?" Scott's warm breath brushed the back of my neck.

I jumped and turned, finding him standing close enough he could steal a kiss before I caught my balance.

He steadied me with an arm around my waist. "Or what?" He repeated, amusement in his voice.

"Or this." I pressed my lips and body to his.

"I definitely pick this." He shifted his weight, leaning his back against my car and taking me with him. "Does that mean you're going to *come* here instead?"

After all this time, a suggestion like that still embarrassed me. But it also coiled with desire in my belly. The conflict wasn't as delicious as I wanted it to be. "Can we be quiet?"

"No. I'd want to make you scream."

"It's a concrete garage. The echo would be terrifying."

Scott tilted his head forward to rest his forehead against mine. "Or orgasmic. Which could be a problem. I can't be sharing that kind of joy with my employees—I have a reputation to maintain."

"Dork."

"Your dork." He glided a hand down my arm to grasp my hand and press my palm to the distinct outline of his cock. "The well-hung one you're about to send on a lonely, lonely business trip."

I shook my head, but didn't pull my hand away. "I'd rather you stay here. Remember that."

"Fine." He huffed out a sigh. "I'll call you when I land."

"You'd better." I stole one more kiss, and patted his ass playfully as he grabbed his bag from my car.

As he walked toward his own SUV, I couldn't help but appreciate the view. I was also dragging my feet. Home was empty. Bri was probably already gone. I should pick up some food, maybe text Riley and ask if she'd seen any good TV shows lately.

My twin's idea of great TV was boys kissing boys, frequently in a foreign language, and tonight that sounded like the perfect thing to binge.

A flash of color out of the corner of my eye caught my attention, and I turned to Bri walking by, her head down. I could let her pass. Call this weekend a fling and move on.

"Bri?" I called out. "Do-you-want-to-have-dinner-with-me?" The question was all-but blurted out and sounded louder than I intended. But I couldn't take it back.

When she focused on me, there was a sadness in her expression that made my heart crack. "I'm not in the mood to be out in public, but thank you," she said.

There was a cloud around her, and I wanted to reach out and wrap her in a hug. "We don't have to go out. We can go back to my place or yours. I can listen." Because I didn't want to see her like this, whatever *this* was. I wanted to help.

ALLYSON LINDT

"This isn't... I can't..." She frowned and turned her gaze to her feet again.

Very unlike the woman I'd been getting to know. "Do you have someone you can talk to? About whatever's going on?"

She let out a sharp laugh, but never smiled. "It's not that kind of thing. I'll deal with it."

"You'll bottle it up because it's hard to face." Been there. Done that. A lot. "At least let me feed you while you're pretending you're not feeling whatever you're feeling." I grabbed her wrist and tugged her toward the passenger side of my car.

"Are you... kidnapping me?"

Technically. I supposed. "Yes. And I'm going to make you eat gas station pizza and ice cream. And I can't make you talk to me, but I can stuff my face so my lips aren't flapping, in case you decide you want to get your thoughts out."

"I don't have a choice in this, do I?" Bri slid into the car without further prompting.

"Nope. Not on the food. Only on the talking." Why was I pushing this? I wouldn't do this for Barb.

But Bri looked like she needed a friend. An ear that came without assumption. And I knew what it was like to need someone who would just listen and to not know where to go.

There was no further argument from Bri as we merged into evening traffic, but there wasn't much of anything else, either. She occasionally tapped her fingers on her leg, but stopped every few minutes.

I wanted to push, but I also understood that wouldn't help her.

A small detour was required to grab dinner, and after about fifteen minutes of inching through the outer reaches of downtown, I'd secured a premade pizza from the convenience store, plus brownie batter ice cream, and a pint of Chubby Hubby.

At the condo, Bri continued the trend of not saying much beyond *please* and *thank you*.

How long should I keep her here before I let her go home? Was I helping at all, having brought her here, or was this a selfish decision so I could have company?

Bri put down her paper plate, a slice of mostly-eaten pizza on it. "My grandfather is dying."

Oh. I'd known the man wasn't doing well, but I hadn't expected this.

"I shouldn't have said that. I don't think anyone is supposed to know," Bri said. "Like, anyone in the business. Can we keep this between us?"

"It's just between us, I promise." I couldn't fathom spreading around details like this.

"Except you'll tell Scott." She gave me a dry smile.

I nodded. "Most likely. But he'll respect your wishes as well."

"Thank you." Bri stuffed another bite of pizza in her mouth, and the silence returned.

I didn't know much about her grandfather. He'd always been a silent investor. Tended to vote with Scott when such a thing was called for. And I knew that Bri's father really wanted that position. *Really* wanted to get his foot in the door at Rinslet and have a say in the direction of the company.

"Dad is trying to make sure I can't say goodbye." Bri set down an empty plate. "He's made sure I can't get into the hospice." Her frown marred her face, and she radiated a kind of frustration I didn't expect from her.

But it was a reasonable response. Why would someone do that? What kind of asshole was Chester Jr.?

Oh, right. I already knew the answer to that.

But… "What if I could help?" How? I was good at making phone calls. Talking to people. That might actually come in handy here. "Where's he staying?"

"I don't know. Dad wouldn't tell me that, but I can tell you where he was before."

"It's a starting place." I took the information from her. It was after six, and most of the normal staff wasn't in, but that worked to my advantage. Each person I talked to, I told them I was a friend of the distraught granddaughter. I promised I didn't want them to get in trouble.

And after about six calls, I'd found two people who took pity on me, one giving me the hospice number and the other letting me make an appointment. I hung up and looked at Bri. "You can go see him tomorrow afternoon."

Her eyes grew wide. "Are you serious?"

"Why would I make that up?"

"Oh, God. Thank you. Thank you so much." The lingering cloud around her seemed to thin, and she smiled for the first time this evening.

I handed her a spoon, and pointed to the ice cream. "Any time. I mean it. Tell me about him?"

We spent the next few hours with her sharing stories about her grandfather, and the tangent leading to so many other things.

"Worst relationship you've ever been in." Why did I say that? What was wrong with me?

Bri's frown was back, full-force. "You don't want to know that."

She was right. What a horrible question to ask. "I do." *Stop it Kenzie.* "I'll go first."

Bri twisted her mouth, but she didn't say anything.

"I was still in college." There was still time to stop this. To not delve into topics that would tear me apart, and—based on her reaction—do the same to Bri. "I met a guy who was all command and confidence and sexiness."

"So you have a type." A hint of teasing slipped into Bri's voice.

I looked her over. "I suppose I do."

A corner of her mouth tugged up.

"Anyway." I started this and now I had to get through it. "I'd taken too many classes that semester, and I was struggling with coursework, on top of making time to be with him, combined with a full time job, and I was drowning in all of it."

Yup. This hurt. I'd moved past it a decade ago, though. "At first he was supportive. Sweet. But his attitude quickly shifted from *it's okay, I know you're busy this weekend* to *if you liked me, you'd make time for me* and *if you were competent, you'd have a handle on all of this.*

Bri's growl startled me. "Fucking... *Grr*."

I couldn't help but be warmed by her reaction. "I know now that it was bad, but back then... I tried so hard to make it work. To prove to him I was *competent*. It nearly wrecked me. If it hadn't been for Riley..." I'd never been more grateful for Riley's ability to say *it's okay to tell the world to fuck off sometimes*.

"I'm sorry." Bri squeezed my knee.

"Thanks. And you don't have to tell me yours if you don't want. I shouldn't have asked."

She drew in a shuddering breath. "No. Fair is fair. It's a short story though."

"I'd still like to hear it."

Bri puffed out her cheeks and exhaled slowly. "I told you that you're not the first married woman I've dated."

"More or less." Oh, crap. That was her worst...?

"I was seeing her and her husband. That was the deal up front. I date them. Both of them. It was all sparks and heat at first. The three of us lit the sheets on fire. Then it started to sink in what this was. I was only allowed to see them, and only at the same time. I wasn't allowed to tell anyone we were all together. It basically became clear they wanted to be able to put me on a shelf when they didn't want me, and pull me out when they did.

"And I wanted their attention so badly, I locked myself away from the rest of my life to get it. I did everything they asked. I nearly destroyed myself trying to fit into their lives." Bri sighed again. "I didn't realize how bad I had it until Manda found me with a bottle of cheap vodka and another of Vallum, and I was trying to figure to the best order to take them in, to make sure it all stayed down."

Oh. "I'm so sorry." What else could I say? I hated the idea that anyone had driven Bri to that, especially people she trusted.

She gave her head a hard shake. "It took me a while, but I mostly dealt with it. The most important thing, I won't let it happen again."

Right. Of course she wouldn't. I didn't blame her.

Eventually we ended up in bed, but it was because it was comfortable. There was no sex, just talking.

This wasn't like what we shared over the weekend, but it was just as potent.

As I fought off tiredness, a whisper of fear formed in the back of my mind—what if I lost this?

TEN
SCOTT

It was an hour later here than back home, and the people who could help me were either not in the office in Salt Lake yet, or were here with me. I needed someone on site at the Rinslet offices.

Until then, I was stuck in a war room, my computer in front of me, and my fingers drumming on the table instead of flying across the keyboard.

I had one option, but I wasn't sure I should exercise it.

According to Kenzie, Bri had not only spent the night at our condo, but was awake and had left an hour ago. She could help. In fact, she was probably perfect for this project. Someone who was intelligent and competent, but had no idea what they were doing when it came to programming.

I needed the opposite of an expert, to help us figure out why this security software kept breaking.

Fuck it. I was using my insider knowledge to call her and find out how long until she was on-site.

She answered quickly, and the background noise was non-existent.

"Are you at your desk?" I asked.

"Yes. I couldn't sleep last night."

Weak ass excuse, but at least she kind of tried. "I know where you actually were. Bad movie sequels—*I know where you slept last night.*" It was a good thing I was alone in here. "I currently care more about what you're up to right now."

"Working? I couldn't sit still at home, and this was my final destination—speaking of movie titles—so I came in to catch up on some admin stuff. Do you need something?"

"I do. I need you to find one of the test machines in the Development room."

"Is it lost?"

I laughed. "Smart ass. Are you there yet?"

"I'm on the elevator. Not all of us can teleport from one place to another."

I let out an exaggerated sigh. "Amateur."

She started humming, and I couldn't quite make out the tune. Though I assumed she was providing elevator music rather than speaking.

"What is that?" It was going to drive me nuts until I figured it out.

"I don't know. Some oldies song."

Fuck me. I knew exactly what it was. "Nirvana. Lithium. That's not old."

"Considering the state of their band, pretty sure they didn't make any new music after the late 1900's."

I glared at the phone, though she couldn't see me. "You're only a decade younger than me."

"A decade is a lifetime."

This was more fun than I expected, but I didn't have a comeback beyond *nuh-uh,* so I shifted to, "Are you there yet?"

She didn't respond to me directly, but I heard muffled voices in the background. That would most likely be Link she was talking to.

"Back," Bri said. "I found the computer. It went out for drinks last night and we discovered it sleeping off a hangover in Elliot's office."

Ludicrous. What a great conversation. "Give it a cookie and tell it it's a good boy."

"Are you projecting? Do you need a cookie and some praise?" Bri's question was full of teasing.

This was way more fun than should be legal on a Friday morning with a half billion dollar project hanging in the balance. "I *need* you to hack into our gaming server, using that computer."

Bri's laugh was loud and clear, and stopped abruptly. "Wait. You're serious. No, you can't be. What do you really need me to do?"

"Hack into our gaming servers," I repeated.

There was a long pause, followed by, "Let me hand you to Link."

"No. Link knows what he's doing."

"I'd be offended, but that's the point I'm trying to make."

I should explain myself. "We have this piece of software that's meant to keep out certain types of online attacks. It's been built by people who know what they're doing, to keep out people who know what they're doing. But it keeps breaking. We can't track down why. We've been through three ethical hacks, and they're finding nitpicky stuff, but they're not filling the hole."

Bri's giggle was softer this time. "Sorry." She sounded anything but.

Was I grateful she couldn't see my grin? I wasn't used to anyone talking to me like this in the office. The conversation with Judith and Elliot the other day was similar, and a fucking HR minefield, but it felt different with Bri. Like she was setting a new bar, and I still had to find where it was. How far I could go. And *God damn* that was intriguing.

"Anyway. My theory is that we're looking at this wrong. It won't just be experts trying to break in. That machine has a system that logs all keystrokes into the new security system, and has the latest version installed, and I want to see if someone who's not familiar with any of it can make it break. There's an icon on the desktop."

"Looks like a little safe?"

"That's it," I confirmed.

"You didn't hide it very well, did you?"

Was she questioning my off-the cuff design decisions?

Fair enough. "We weren't trying to hide it."

"I'm just saying, if I were putting a login to a secret system on a computer, I'd make the icon... I don't know... maybe an image that said *Standardization Protocol* or something."

ALLYSON LINDT

That'd definitely keep *me* from clicking it. "I'll take that under advisement. Click that icon."

"Oops."

"How do you *oops* already?"

"I clicked the icon next to it while you were talking. I wanted to see what *Nude Skins* was."

What? "What is it?"

"Nude skins. Characters with no clothes." Bri was amused.

This must have to do with Elliot and Judith's conversation from the other day. "At least whoever put it there has a solid understanding of labeling icons so they're easily understood."

"Uh-huh." Bri sounded distracted or uninterested—it was hard to tell which. "Are our characters really this well built under their clothing?"

Great. Now I had an admin looking at digital porn. "Yes. We have good artists. Close that and open the safe icon?"

"Okay." She let out a loud huff.

Thank God she didn't call me Daddy. I might've liked that.

"Are you looking at a login screen?" I asked.

"Yes."

"Try to log in."

"Like with my username and password from the network? Yours? Is the password *Password*?"

She was all sass all the time, apparently. I liked this.

"This is the part you figure out on your own," I said. "I want you to do whatever you think might get you in."

"This is nothing like those hacker movies."

"I fucking hope not." I kept half an eye on the keylogger attached to the system, and made a mental note to check the logs and see if Elliot turned them off to put the nude models on that system. He and I would talk about that... Later.

There was some silence. Some breathing.

I wanted to ask Bri how things were going with Kenzie. What Bri thought of the entire relationship.

And a sharp realization made me realize that was the line. That point I couldn't cross. Not at work.

That sucked. Wasn't I supposed to be in a position without restrictions on things? Hadn't I built myself a job where I didn't have to hold back?

Yeah, right. I knew better than that.

This wasn't just about me. It involved Kenzie. Bri. If I asked the wrong thing, if the wrong person heard, if someone decided I was using this to manipulate her job—

The screen with the keylogger data flooded with gibberish, and a loud beep carried through the phone from Bri's end.

"What did you do?" I couldn't hide my excitement.

"I... I took screen shots of the nude models and pasted them into the username and password boxes."

"What? Why?" Link's loud question came from the background.

It was perfect. "You're a fucking genius. Let me talk to Link."

Bri's, "For you. Scott," was muffled.

"What is this?" Link came on the line a moment later.

It was exactly what we'd missed. A rookie overlook, and a huge security hole. "She overloaded the buffer with raster and metadata."

"Why would she do that?"

I explained my plan to Link, and he seemed to follow, though he didn't seem to have the same enthusiasm for the discovery.

"Bring everything offline," I said to him. "Restore the system to this morning's mirror, and tell Elliot to take his computerized porn off, then create a new mirror. Oh, and give the phone back to Bri."

"On it, boss."

Great thing about Link—he was smart, he was efficient, and he'd tell me if he thought any of this was a mistake. Otherwise, he'd do the job.

"I take it that worked?" Bri sounded uncertain when she came back on the phone,

"Perfectly. Thank you so much. Lunch is on me."

"Fuck yeah. I'm splurging for extra cheese on my Big Mac."

No wonder Kenzie liked spending time with her. I had to take this seriously for just a moment, though. "Kenzie swore me to secrecy, but good luck this afternoon." I'd heard about Chester Sr. I'd deal with the business side of it separately. This was about making sure Bri was okay.

"Thank you…. Hang on." Bri went silent for a moment, but I swore I heard the shuffle of footsteps. "Back. I had to find someplace private. I wanted to say thank you."

"For what?"

"For not keeping Kenzie to yourself."

The words were simple. Sincere.

And they hit hard. Harder than expected. Harder than I knew how to deal with. Why couldn't I process my response? "Of course." I couldn't force the same emotion into my voice that had been there a moment earlier. "I need to get back to work."

As I disconnected, Bri's final words stuck in my head.

Why?

ELEVEN
BRIENNE

Thank you. For not keeping Kenzie to yourself.

I shouldn't have said that. Not for Scott's sake, but for my own.

Why did I think I needed to say that?

That wasn't the only part of the conversation with Scott that lingered in my head for reasons I couldn't explain. It was a simple work call. Fun, but I had fun with a lot of the people here—if I didn't the job wouldn't be worth it.

Thoughts of him mingled with last night. How sweet Kenzie was. How she was able to work actual magic with the phone calls she made. No one else would do something like that for me except Manda, but that wasn't her skill set. She'd be more likely to sketch me up the perfect tattoo to help me deal with the disappointment of not being able to do more about my Grandpa.

As if summoned by the thought, a text from Manda popped up on my phone. *Having lunch at that sandwich place near your office. Join me?*

Talking to her, out loud, sounded like the perfect way to climb out of my own head. I replied with, *Be there soon.*

Less than fifteen minutes later, I was sitting across from Manda, next to a window overlooking the street.

"Are you dealing okay with the whole gossip thing? About everyone knowing you're actually Daddy Asshole's secret daughter?" Manda asked.

I couldn't help but smirk at the nickname, the same way I did every time she mentioned my father. "Actually, aside from Day One, there hasn't been anything to deal with. The news about who I was and who I worked for and who I had dinner with kind of faded. Just like..." *huh.*

"Like what?"

"Like Scott said it would." I don't know why I was surprised. Maybe because I'd expected the news to be such a big deal and then it vanished like nothing. Neat trick.

"So Scott's not the wicked monster Chester Jr. makes him out to be?" Manda teased.

After that phone call this morning? That random, weird, so much fun call? Considering that he'd married an incredible woman. "No. He's not any kind of monster."

"What was that?" Manda studied me.

"What was what?"

"That dopey look when you talk about your boss."

I didn't. I wasn't. "There was no dopey look." Could I tell her? I told her everything else, but I'd been so focused on keeping this secret...

Manda gave me another look. "You definitely look goofy when you talk about Scott."

"Okay, so I have to tell you something and you have to swear not to tell *anyone*. Like this is so much a secret, it never goes beyond here." Except now that I had the chance to talk about this, I was bursting to share the news. I needed to stop being melodramatic. Besides, Manda would get along great with Kenzie.

Because this wasn't about him, it was about her. He just reminded me of her.

Manda watched me with expectation. "Are you being melodramatic right now?"

"Am I ever?"

"Last Friday, when you had to go to that party? Two weeks ago when you couldn't get a hold of your tattoo artist. A month ago—"

Fine. "Okay, sometimes I'm melodramatic. But this time… Promise me first."

"I swear. Cross my heart. You know you can trust me."

It was now or never. I had to talk this out with *someone*. "So, I'm um… kind of seeing… the boss's wife."

"You're *seeing*—"

I reached across the table and clapped my hand over her mouth when her voice rose.

"Between us," I hissed.

Manda peeled my fingers away from her face and leaned in. "Are you fucking with me right now? Are you an idiot? I thought you loved this job. What do you do when he finds out?"

"He already knows."

"Oh. *Oh.* No, Bri. You can't… Not for any job. How long have they been making you do this?"

"*No.*" I didn't blame her for jumping to conclusions. I'd dated a couple that really didn't treat me… It was a bad relationship. "I learned from last time. This is different." Was that part of why it was as terrifying as it was incredible?

"So, you're good with it and they're both good with it," Manda said.

Exactly. "She's so much fun. You'll love her. She's kind of sheltered, but she's trying to break out, and, *Oh my God*, Manda. It's amazing." Wait. Was I gushing? About Kenzie? *Fuck.*

One corner of Manda's mouth pulled up, but her eyes were guarded. "If they hurt you, I'll hurt them."

I raised my brows. "Are you done?"

"If you're happy, I'm super happy for you." She finally grinned. "*Oh.* You should bring your new girl to the Red Faire in a few weeks. Her guy too if he wants."

I loved that idea. With two tiny issues. "She's not *my girl* and it's supposed to be a secret."

Manda's scowl was back. "How good can it be if you're not allowed to tell anyone?"

"It's complicated." It wasn't that I was a secret. But the whole thing… "You know there's more to it."

"I think I know, but it's a fine line, Bri. How about, if you can keep your hands off each other, come as *friends.*"

I was looking forward to Ren Faire, and introducing Kenzie to Manda, and…

"Now you're frowning." Manda nudged my fingers.

Because if I kept seeing Kenzie, would it always be like this? Okay, so it had only been a week, and I shouldn't even be thinking of what I had with her as long term, but suddenly the idea of hiding this long term sat heavily in my gut. "Nope. I'm good. I'll see if she wants to come."

Manda didn't look convinced, but she let me change the subject to a new tattoo I was thinking about getting. Before I knew it, lunch was over and I had to get back to work.

If they hurt you, I'll hurt them, Manda's words echoed in my head as I returned to my desk. It didn't matter, because I wasn't going to get close enough to Kenzie or Scott for *hurt* to be an option.

This was still just fun. I had control of things.

Which is why when Kenzie called me an hour or so later, my heart did a little happy dance at seeing her name on my cell phone.

Calm the fuck down, bitch. I took a deep breath. "Yellow," I answered with the same bright tone I'd give any friend.

"Hey, you." Kenzie's simple greeting sent a tingle racing over me. "I was wondering if you'd like company this afternoon."

"I can't ask you to do that."

"I really don't mind. I'm free, and I can wait in the car unless you need me."

I've got this, really. The words lodged in my throat. Having a friend with me when I went to see Grandpa, someone who could squeeze my hand before I went in, and tell people I was allowed to be there if anyone tried to stop me, sounded nice. "That would be wonderful, thank you."

She picked me up a short while later, to drive me to the hospice. Leaving work early on a Friday was supposed to be a fun thing. A little wicked, with a reason to look forward to what came next.

Instead, I was thinking about a week ago. Grandpa called me. It had been a simple conversation, and he sounded tired, but he'd been in good spirits when he asked me to attend the investor party in his place.

I'd had no idea he was so close to death.

And now he was—

The only family I had left. He'd be gone soon. The one person who believed I was more than a disappointment. More than a doll to be traded as needed.

I tried to push aside the thoughts, but they clawed at my mind in a way I hadn't struggled with for a long time.

When Kenzie squeezed my hand, it jarred me from the thoughts. "We're here," she said.

So we were. In front of a brick and stone building that looked deceptively unimpressive.

"Do you want me to come in with you?" Kenzie asked.

Yes. "No. I'll be fine, thank you. I'll try not to take too long."

"Take as long as you need." She gave my hand another squeeze.

I stepped from the car, and as I walked toward the building, I summoned a wall of resilience, adding

99

another brick with each new step. I had no idea what I was heading into, but whatever it was, I could face it.

Inside looked a lot like a nice hospital waiting room. Neutral carpet, beige walls, and a front desk with a fresh bouquet of flowers at one corner.

The woman behind the counter gave me a warm smile. "How can I help you?"

"I'm Brienne Walker. I'm here to see my grandfather, Chester?" This was the first *test*. Would she call security now that she knew my name?

"Of course. Have a seat and someone will be right with you."

I perched on the edge of a nearby chair, and tried to lose myself in the fish swimming in a tank on one of the walls. The vibrant colors and lazy moments should've been calming, but my mind raced too fast for me to grasp anything, especially peace.

A door latched open, startling me, and a man in scrubs stepped into the room. "Ms. Walker? This way."

I was in. This might have called for a victory dance, but the mood wasn't right. The wide halls and speckled white added to the hospital feeling. I kept half an ear on the nurse's instructions about not exciting Grandpa too much. How to call for help if needed, and more.

"Can I hug him?" I heard myself ask.

"Of course." The nurse stopped in front of a room and opened the door. "I'll be nearby if you need. We also have a witness and notary on staff, if that comes up."

"Thank you." I stepped into the room.

When I saw Grandpa, my heart sank. He looked

small in the bed. Nearly the same color as the white pillowcase, and his skin a similar texture. How did this happen? How did I miss that he was fading?

His smile was warm when he saw me. "Hi, Princess."

"Hi, Grandpa." I tried to be careful wrapping him in a hug, but he felt so frail under my touch that I worried I might break him. I stepped back from the bed, not sure what to do with myself. "How are you?" Right. Dying.

"As good as ever," he said despite my dumb question. "You look good. Been breaking hearts and wrecking portfolios?"

"Every chance I get."

"That's my girl." He sighed. "I want you to tell me all about what you've been up to. All of it. However, I don't always stay awake long, and I have to get the business out of the way first, in case I fade fast."

Right. I should've expected that. But at least business with Grandpa wasn't the same as with Dad. "What business?"

His chuckle was dry and papery, but filled with amusement. What was he up to? "I'm leaving you everything, Princess. The companies are already structured to be run by the people in charge, but the money, the house, the board seat at Rinslet, they all go to you."

"I don't want it." The words tumbled out with little thought. It was true though. I wanted my grandfather. Not his things.

"Then you can make that decision when it's yours. Just don't let your father have it."

Spiteful old man. I did love him. I also wasn't going to argue with him; not when he was like this. "Okay."

"Do you have your phone with you?"

I pulled it from my bag. "Yes."

"Good. The paperwork is already notarized. Most of this will go into effect after I'm gone. However, you'll need to take over the board seat immediately."

What? No. "Scott has your vote. Why—?"

"Your father will fight me on this. You know that. This helps minimize that argument. Get your father and Mr. McAllister on the line."

I didn't—

"Please, Princess."

I wasn't used to hearing Grandpa ask for anything. His world, everything was expected. Demanded. Taken. I wanted to argue this, but I didn't want to waste what little time I had with him on a fight like that. I did what he asked, calling Scott first and getting him to wait while I got Dad on the phone as well.

The conversation with the three of them was a blur. It had to be, or I'd lose my grasp on anything keeping me together. Especially when Scott said he was grateful to see someone like me in this position, and Dad countered that it was an idiot decision and I'd only fuck everything up.

Fuck him. I may not want this, but if Dad did, I was keeping it.

Besides, there was something intoxicating about putting myself at the same level as Scott in anything.

In the background of Scott's end of the call, there was chatter about security and firewalls. I didn't understand most of it, but it was easier to listen to than Dad slinging insults and Scott countering them.

We wrapped up the call, and I spent the next little while catching up with Grandpa. Hearing his stories about which patients were flirting with him, and telling him my tales about some of the tattoos he hadn't seen yet.

He tired out quickly, though. As he faded off in the middle of the conversation, I made sure he was comfortable, and headed outside.

I was both grateful Kenzie was still waiting, and hated that I couldn't do this alone. I slid into her car.

"How'd it go?" Her voice was kind.

"You don't already know?"

She gave me a half-smile. "I know about the business stuff. I want to know about the important things though. Do you want to go back to my place and talk?"

"So you don't have to sleep alone?" I was trying so hard not to feel.

Kenzie shook her head once. "So you don't have to."

TWELVE

BRIENNE

IT WAS ALL BUT PITCH-BLACK IN THE ROOM WHEN I WOKE up. Kenzie slept soundly next to me, but something had jarred me from sleep.

The clock on the nightstand said it was a little after one in the morning. Why was I already making a habit of sleeping here? It had been a little odd, crawling into bed, knowing that Kenzie usually shared this space with someone besides me, but it didn't take me long to get over the weirdness.

Mostly because I liked her company so much. It wasn't the same as with Manda, though it was hard to describe how it was different. I'd go out drinking with either of them. Gossip into the night. I didn't quite trust Kenzie with my darkest secrets, but I could see it happening.

That was terrifying on its own. Hearing myself admit that.

And with Kenzie, I wanted to cuddle, too. I wanted

to wrap myself around her and wrap myself up in her, and—

There was another noise. It came from the other side of the bedroom door.

I pulled on my leggings, so I didn't give a potential burglar a free show of me in my T-shirt and panties, and tiptoed from the room. The living room was empty, but a gray light peeked from under the kitchen door, and I swore I heard a light *tip tap* coming from the other side.

Pushing into the kitchen, I stopped short when I realized Scott was sitting on one of the stools at the bar. "Oh. I didn't expect… you." That was super smart of me. Not.

He looked up from his laptop with a smirk. "You know I live here."

"Yes, but…" *I thought you were halfway across the country.*

"I managed to catch a flight back tonight," Scott said. "But I came home to find two people already in my bed."

Right. "Oops."

"Don't feel bad unless you did it by mistake." Was that a catch in his voice? "That's not why you're awake is it?" No, that was teasing. Like he so frequently did.

"I heard a noise and came to investigate."

He nodded, as if in approval. "It's good to know Kenzie has a guard kitten while I'm gone."

This was so odd. It was easiest enough in theory to say *I'm hooking up with the boss's wife and he knows*, but standing here talking to him like it was no big deal…

I guess I hadn't been prepared for it to be so easy. I also wasn't prepared for the way his calling me *kitten* sent pleasant shivers down my spine. Not that he meant it that way or that I should take it that way, and not that there was permanence in any of this.

Was there? "What are you working on? The Nashville stuff still?"

"No. We wrapped that up. It's ready for the announcement at SXSW, thanks to you." He glanced at his screen, and twisted his mouth. "I'm trying to decide if I want to write a memoir. Would you like to read the first page?"

Of course. "Yes. Definitely."

He turned the screen toward me.

It was a document that said *Chapter One* at the top, and nothing else.

Chloe was a writer. She had the game writers underneath her. So I knew there was a mile-long list of things I shouldn't say in a situation like this. "It's a great start."

Scott snorted. "Super diplomatic of you."

"What has you stalled?"

He took the laptop back, and patted the seat next to him. "I need coffee. Do you want some?"

"Not if I'm going back to sleep tonight. Thank you, though." I sat, and he stood to move around the counter.

"I don't know where to start." Scott made minimal sound as he moved through the kitchen, from filling the coffee pot to dumping in ground coffee. He'd done this late-night thing more than once. "I'm running out of time to decide if I want to sign the contract or not, and I can't figure out if it's a good idea."

"You've been offered a contract for this?" I was

surprised. From what I knew about publishing, that wasn't the kind of thing that was just handed out for a book that didn't exist at all. "They must've pursued you for a reason. A better reason than you're successful and handsome."

He raised an eyebrow, grabbed two mugs out of the cupboard, and dropped two tea bags in the second one. "You're pretty incredible to look at yourself."

Another shiver of desire raced down my spine. I wasn't doing this. Sure, I tended to laugh in the face of decorum, and biting my tongue wasn't for me, but there was a mile long list of reasons to not flirt with this man.

"Is this how you landed the deal? You talked pretty to the editor?" I meant the question to be light. Playful. Instead, my voice came out husky.

I cleared my throat with a cough.

"No. I save the pretty talk for special occasions." He filled an electric kettle and turned it on. This kitchen had everything. "I was at a party, and telling someone the story of how I got from high school to here. A group of people gathered to listen, and one of them was an editor with one of the big publishers. We chatted, they drew up an offer, and now here I am, staring at a blank screen and wondering if I can figure out how to write a book."

I'd heard Scott tell stories—pretty much anyone who'd ever been in a meeting with him, at a party with him, anywhere with him, had. He had a knack for spinning real life into something extraordinary. "So take all those things you say out loud and write them down. They can be edited from there."

"It doesn't work that way."

"Why not?"

"The story is never the same twice. I adapt, based on the audience."

I feigned shock. "Does that mean you lie?"

"It's an embellishment." He looked amused. "Do you tell the story of your childhood the same every time?"

Did he realize the nerve he struck with that question? Something made me think he might. "I don't tell the story of my childhood. Especially not in business settings." Because most professionals didn't like to hear the less-than-professional things I had to say about my father.

"Maybe someday you'll tell me."

My *not likely* stuck in my throat.

Scott poured water into the cup with tea bags and slid it to me, along with a bowl of sugar cubes. He poured himself coffee and returned to his seat.

How did he know I liked lavender tea?

"I hope that's all right." He adjusted his stool enough that he could face me, but he didn't pull back far enough to keep his knees from brushing mine. "That's what Kenzie likes, so it's what we have."

"It's great. Thank you." I waited in silence for my drink to steep. Did I ruin the conversation? Why weren't we talking? Why wasn't *he* talking? "Maybe you could tell *me* your story, I'll write it down, and then you'll have an audience of one."

"I appreciate the offer, but it's not the same." He

sipped his coffee. "You're not a businessman looking for a quick *ooh* and *ahh* followed by a sharp punchline."

"You say that like it's a bad thing." To be fair, in my world it always had been, especially with my father's associates.

"Not at all. But you deserve more than a quick *ooh* and *ahh*."

And now he was flirting again. Or did I just want him to be?

I grabbed his laptop to set it in front of me, and rested my fingers over the home keys. "You can't edit a blank page."

"Not sure that's true."

"Assume it is until you learn otherwise. Talk."

"Where do I start?"

"Wherever the story takes you. It doesn't have to be the beginning. Say the words and I'll type them."

"Rule breaker. I like it." Scott leaned in on the counter.

"Have you met many people like me who were rule followers?" As in, my dreadlocks, the tattoos, the overall attitude...

Scott raised an eyebrow. "I haven't met anyone else like you."

Fuck me. Anyone else, and I'd definitely call this flirting. And here, with the rest of the world blacked out, with only us, and with how close he sat, an intensity raced through me. My blood roared and my pulse hammered in my ears, and I struggled between *it could be fun* and *back off. You can't do this with him.*

I wasn't doing anything but helping him get his story on the page.

"Okay, picture this." Scott swept one hand across the air, like highlighting a sign or banner. "It's Saturday morning, downtown. Crowded coffee shop. *Loud.* I was playing something handheld. Couldn't even tell you what. It was retro, even five years ago."

I typed as he talked, but this wasn't quite a compelling story.

"This gorgeous blonde approaches me. I'd seen her before. Kind of uptight looking, but brilliant blue eyes. You know exactly what I'm talking about." He winked at me.

I did know, both generically and specifically. He was describing Kenzie. "Let's say I do."

"She asked if she could share my table, and then she read. She had me for company, and she started reading some romancey book instead."

"The nerve." I couldn't summon anything but amusement at his fake disapproval. "What did you do?"

"I asked her about the book, I eventually walked her outside, and of course she was completely enamored with how amazing I was."

"Of course." I should be writing this down. Why was I watching Scott instead?

He was closer now—when did he move around the counter? His arm pressed against mine. His face not much farther away. "She was captivating. Wind blowing her hair in her face. The way she was laughing. Everything about her."

I knew exactly what Scott was talking about. With

Kenzie and with him. It was impossible to pull my gaze away.

"And then the rain started falling." His voice was lower. Deeper.

Why was this drawing me in? I hated men like this. Arrogant. Thought they were God's gift to women. And I wanted him to keep talking. "Are you seriously hitting on me with the story of how you met your wife?" I wanted that to be disgust in my question, but it was curiosity and challenge.

"I am."

"Fucking ballsy."

"No one gets where I am without being ballsy. Do you even know me?"

I really didn't, and I desperately hated myself for wanting to.

"This is different than back then." His voice was rough and the way he studied me made my breath catch.

I swore there was uncertainty in his gaze. "No rain?" I asked.

"No interruption."

As if summoned, behind him, the kitchen door swung open, and Kenzie walked into the room. She stalled, eyes wide and jaw open, when she saw us.

My stomach sank.

THIRTEEN
KENZIE

MY BRAIN WAS STALLED. MY EYES WERE GLUED ON THE scene in front of me. Scott was so close to Bri, they were all but kissing, and the way Bri watched me, she looked like she'd been caught with her hand in the cookie jar.

Or my husband's pants.

No. That was going too far. Open marriage, right? Except she was mine. He was mine. I didn't like the jealousy surging inside and at the same time, I couldn't move around it.

"I knew this was a mistake." Bri hopped from her seat and took several steps back.

Scott spun to face me. "Hey. I missed you." He frowned and turned to Bri again. "A mistake?"

"You'd call it something else?" Her tone was cool.

"I'm not anyone's regret," Scott said.

This was surreal. I was trapped in a sitcom. Or The Twilight Zone.

"Maybe you should get used to disappointments." Bri's tone wasn't as hard as she probably meant it to be.

She looked at me again. Watched me as she approached. "We need to talk about this."

"Kenz?" Scott searched my face.

I couldn't find my voice or anything but disbelief and anger. I wanted to scream at Bri to get the fuck out. Wanted to scream at Scott *how dare you*?

How dare he what? We'd agreed we could see other people. I had been, and now I was going to get upset at him for doing the same?

My focus landed on Bri. "I thought you were mine." The soft words tumbled past my lips before I could stop them.

"I thought this was open. You're married." Bri didn't sound angry. More… confused?

"To *him*." I nodded at Scott.

Scott reached for my hand. "She's right. We should talk about this."

I couldn't. Not right now. I'd say something I'd regret, or possibly just as bad, I'd stop myself from saying something, and then regret that. "No, we shouldn't. I'll go. The two of you can stay. Do whatever you want."

It didn't matter that I was barely dressed. My coat was long enough to keep me warm. A nearby pair of ballet flats were easy to slip on. I didn't know if I was upset or if I'd be okay, I just knew I couldn't be here.

I grabbed my purse and keys, ignoring Scott's and Bri's pleas to stop, and I walked out the door.

The two of them… Was this the first time? They had chemistry. Visible sparks.

Which should be great but also twisted my insides into knots.

This was supposed to be my chance at self-discovery.

I climbed into my car and pointed it in a random direction.

My marriage with Scott, we were allowed to see other people. Bri was allowed to see other people. I couldn't demand neither of them do that, when I still wanted to be with them both.

But the two of them together...

Led me in a circle back to the first thought. Was there already more between them and I hadn't seen it?

Wherever I was going, it couldn't be anyplace that reminded me of Scott. Which was basically everywhere.

This should hurt a lot more, shouldn't it? My heart hadn't caught up to my head—when they fell into sync, this would ache like nobody's business.

Where was the anger? I should feel that, right? That was how people felt when they found their spouse with someone else.

Except Scott came home earlier tonight and found me asleep next to someone else in the bed I shared with him. I was upset because the two of them were standing close to each other and talking in hushed voices.

Damn it.

I pulled into a 24 hour diner I used to go to in high school with Riley. There were no Scott memories here. I'd only been to this place with my sister and our friends. My *friends*. They were judgmental. Harsh. Gossipy.

Nothing like Bri. What if I'd had a friend like Bri in

high school? Someone who owned who she was instead of going with the crowd?

My mother would've hated that. She'd had a hard enough time with the thin streak of rebellion in Riley.

Would Scott have liked me as much if I'd been different when I was younger? He liked Bri.

I was going to drive myself insane if I kept running in circles. Instead, I headed into the diner.

The waiter was a few years younger than me, and he greeted me with a bright smile. "Hey. Alone tonight?" he asked.

Super friendly way to greet me, and any other night I'd think it was great. Tonight, it added to my jumbled thoughts. "Yeah. Alone."

"Take a seat. Coffee?"

"Diet Coke." I headed toward the booth Riley and I always used to sit at.

The waiter was back a moment later, setting my drink in front of me. He handed me a menu. "Mixing it up tonight, or do you want your usual?"

What? "I think you have me confused with someone else."

"Not unless you have a twin."

"I do."

He laughed. "She's got a big husband, looks like he's former military and randomly speaks Russian?"

That would be Zane. "He was Air Force." That meant Riley still came here. Late enough that the overnight waiter knew her. Riley and Zane. She was still living life, the same way she had been before she got married. And I was sitting at home, waiting for the world to do something for me. Bri was supposed to be my way to start exploring and now...

"What's her usual?" I grabbed my phone and showed him a picture of me with Riley. For some reason I felt like I needed to prove it was true.

"Too cool. She gets the coffee plus a cup of hot cocoa and she mixes them together. Strawberry crepes, extra syrup and whipped cream."

That sounded disgustingly sweet and designed to keep someone up all night. "I'll have the same."

"You got it."

Before he could walk away, the front door opened again, and Scott and Bri walked in.

Fuck. "How did you know I was here?" I asked.

They crossed the dining room together. "We followed you," Scott said.

But I'd been in here for a few minutes. "Did you pause to make out in the parking lot before coming in to find me?" Ouch, me.

I wasn't taking it back, though.

"We paused to argue about whether he should talk to you alone or if I should come in with him," Bri said.

"I won," Scott added.

He always did. "You always do."

Scott frowned. "Not true."

I didn't want to fight. Not in public. Not at home. But here I'd feel awkward if I made a scene, and Scott knew that. Not that he was above it anyway.

"New friends." The waiter gave a nervous laugh. "What are you both having? Drinks? Do you need a menu?"

Scott slid into the seat across from me. "I'll have what she's having."

"So I've seen."

"I really should go." Bri stepped back.

You really should. I didn't want to say that.

I shouldn't have gone down this path with her a week ago. I made a mistake enjoying the last few days, loving the last week with Bri. "Stay." I heard myself saying.

"Iced tea. Order of fries," Bri said, but she didn't sit.

I grasped her hand and pulled her to sit next to me.

The silence that settled in was more awkward than the not-quite argument we'd managed to stretch from the condo to here, and I was grateful when the waiter brought back our drinks.

"What's this?" Scott eyed the two mugs in front of him, and the coffee carafe.

"Apparently it's Riley's usual. We're supposed to mix it together." Speaking of Riley, what would she do in my shoes?

Technically, trying to be more like Riley was how I met Scott.

But I didn't want to be like Riley. I loved my sister, but we fought our entire lives to be recognized as individuals.

"What now?" Bri asked.

I didn't know.

FOURTEEN
SCOTT

For a while, I'd seen Kenzie fighting with herself. She was quiet about it, to the point where I wasn't sure she'd put it into words. From the outside it was almost like she'd lost her place in the world, and I didn't know how to help her.

I'd move mountains for her. I'd give her anything she asked for.

At the same time, what she was doing now wasn't her answer. That wouldn't be up to me, except that it involved me.

When we talked about opening our relationship, I hadn't considered exploring on my own. I did a lot of that when I was younger, and Kenzie hadn't had the same chance. But the option was supposed to be there for me.

Suddenly this had become that she could see who she wanted and I couldn't?

Sure, there were half a dozen reasons that person

shouldn't be Bri, but Kenzie shouldn't be one of those reasons.

"I'm sorry I hurt you." I caught Kenzie's gaze and held it as I poured sincerity into my words. "I won't take it back, though."

The way her jaw clenched and her eyes tightened said *I'm going to fight you on this* without her saying a word. That look was one of the reasons I fell for her.

"We were talking," Bri said. "And it was fun. I'm sorry, Kenzie, you don't get to define for me how I do that."

This wasn't how I wanted this to go. I didn't want Kenzie to feel ganged up on. The way she twisted her fingers and pulled them apart meant she was fighting an internal battle and she didn't know if she could share.

"Nothing happened." It wasn't an excuse on my part —it was the truth.

"Something would've," Bri said.

Kenzie's nostrils flared.

If she shut down before we talked about this, nothing we said mattered. Why couldn't I just say *she's hot, you're hot, let's move on?* "None of this changes how I feel about you Kenz. Not now or ever. Another person doesn't have the power to make me stop loving you." I reached for her fingers, and she didn't pull away.

"I know that. I do." Finally, she spoke. Something not argumentative. "But." She let out a long sigh and flipped her hand over, so her palm met mine. She reached for Bri with her other hand, and looked at her. "You're everything I'm not. The two of you are so much alike. You've even got similar childhoods. I bet if he dared you to go skinny dipping in the cruise ship pool at midnight, you'd say *yes*."

That was two years ago. I'd stopped thinking about that moment after she turned me down. Sometimes she said *yes* to my random ideas and sometimes she didn't. Did she linger on every *no*?

Bri grimaced. "I absolutely would not do that. Cruise ship pools are more pee than they are water."

Fuck it all, this was why I was having fun with her. "Some people like that. And there are showers."

"Gross." Bri wrinkled her nose.

Kenzie sighed again. "This is what scares me. The two of you... The chemistry..."

"You and I have that too." Bri kissed the back of Kenzie's knuckles.

It was weird to see that. To not just hear about it, but to watch how natural that was between the women. I should be jealous. "I like that."

"Two women kissing?" Bri didn't look impressed. "I can send you to a few sites."

This wasn't a pornographic thing. It could be, but... "I meant that someone sees the same things in Kenzie that I do."

Pink spread across Kenzie's cheeks,

I squeezed her hand. "Can we all go back to being... whatever we are again?"

"What are we?" Kenzie asked.

Fair question. Friends? Lovers? Weird associates? I had no idea.

"I'll tell you what I'm not." This time it was Bri who

pulled away. "I'm not a doll to be used for your marriage problems."

She thought—? Fuck.

"No. I promise that's not it." Kenzie assured her quickly.

Bri gave a curt nod. She may not be completely convinced. "And I'm not dating the boss and his wife. So. Bad. So many complications."

"Technically not an issue anymore," I said. Not since she was on our board of directors.

Bri's snort was derisive. "You think that'll fly? Me saying *Hi, I'm the newest board member, and guess who I'm boinking?*"

"Boinking. I like it." The creases in Kenzie's forehead were fading.

It was a fun word, but not accurate. "You're not though, Bri. Not me. We didn't even kiss."

"You would have." Kenzie didn't sound upset now.

"Probably." I'd certainly been picturing it. "Are you okay with that?"

Kenzie nodded. "I'm getting there."

Bri grabbed a fry from her plate. "You feeling better enough to eat?" She dipped the fry in some of the cream cheese mixture spilling from one of Kenzie's crepes.

Kenzie eyed the food. "Is that good?"

"I don't know. It's sweet and salty, so it should be, right?" Bri held it toward her.

It always worked for me. And I was captivated by what I was watching. Kenzie flicking her tongue along the long thick fry with the cream dripping from it. That was completely phallic, and I was captivated.

"It's good." Kenzie leaned in, close to Bri, when she was done.

I couldn't stop staring, and my cock didn't care that the argument wasn't over. Fucking hell, that didn't have any right to be so hot. "You have no idea."

Kenzie's blush deepened and Bri laughed. The tension around us loosened and cracked.

Kenzie's chest rose and fell with her deep breath. "I'm glad we talked about this, and I'm glad you stayed, Bri." Her tone was softer. Less argumentative.

"Me too," Bri said.

Was that that? Were we good?

"How was your trip, Scott?" Kenzie looked at me.

Apparently we were good. I suspected this would come up again, but no reason to beat it into the ground if we were moving on. I downed a long swallow of the coffee and hot chocolate mixture—it actually wasn't bad. A little sweet, but still good.

"It was fascinating until it wasn't. We're good to go with the project." The words left a hollow pit in my chest, because it meant the challenge and newness was over.

"Time for the next big thing, right?" Bri asked. "Like making a new game?"

Yes.

Kenzie looked between us. "Isn't that what you do all the time? Make new games?"

Not in the way Bri meant. "She's talking about *new*

new." Like what Elliot and Judith had been discussing. "I can't. Not that way."

"Why not? You're the boss." Bri made it sound like that was the solution to every issue. As if she didn't know better.

And yet, I didn't have a good counter for her. "I need a different boss to tell me what gets dropped instead to make it happen." Like *just stop making the series defining titles that made your brand what it is, and risk it all by switching to something new and fun and fascinating and rule breaking and—*

"You know someone who can tell you to do that." Kenzie jerked her head at Bri.

I laughed, because it was easier to brush this off than slip into the part of me that wanted it. "Still doesn't work that way." Fuck, I wished it worked that way.

I didn't want to follow this conversation, because it was a problem I didn't have a solution to. I hated those, and this was the worst one yet.

Instead, I grabbed a stern voice and focused on Bri. "Are you the one who scribbled all over my wife?"

"Not scribbled. Created stunning art, and yes, that was me." Bri smirked.

Kenzie's fingers flew toward her shoulder blade, where the henna under her shirt was fading, but still looked sexy. "She almost has me convinced to get a real one."

Did I like that idea? Yeah, I did.

"Are you leaning toward something specific?" Bri asked.

"I thought I'd see if Riley could draw me something, but I don't know what yet."

Ooh, brainstorming time. I grabbed a napkin, and a crayon from the little box next to the ketchup, and I sketched out a series of lines.

Bri twisted her head and examined the drawing ."Is that a puzzle box?"

"Are you trying to Hellraiser me?" Kenzie sounded concerned.

Sigh. "It's a circuit board."

Bri took the napkin from me and turned it over. She sketched out a pair of wings as best she could, given the paper was tearing.

"Aren't angel wings kind of cliche?" Kenzie asked.

Bri shook her head. "Not if you're an angel."

"Fucking smooth." I didn't mean to say that out loud, but I was impressed. "Nice."

A corner of Bri's mouth tugged up. "You think so? I wasn't trying to flirt or anything."

"That's what makes it work. It shows when you force it." The look Kenzie shot me was hard to decipher.

Or I just didn't want to. "I don't force anything. I'm this charming naturally."

The conversation continued to flow as we finished our food. This all felt good. Right. As we were ready to go, I said, "Leave your car here, Kenz. We'll grab it tomorrow."

"Do you like abandoning cars?" Bri teased.

She meant like we had with hers at the resort. Was that really only a week ago? "I like keeping the important people close."

The conversation didn't pause as the three of us headed home, with Bri leaning forward between the seats to talk to Kenzie and me.

It was after three when we walked through the front door, and I was high strung and wired. I had no idea how to harness this energy, but I needed to figure some of it out.

"Are we all good?" Bri asked after we hung up our coats and the three of us moved toward the couch.

"Yeah. We're good," Kenzie said. "All of it. Whatever happens next happens."

"Thank God." Bri stepped in my path.

I pulled up short, and my entire body sparked to life when she draped her arms around my neck.

She tilted her head up and brushed her lips over mine. This wasn't a sweet, tentative peck. The way she dragged her tongue across my bottom lip before she pulled away was a challenge, and her full body pressed to mine.

There was no way this was going unanswered, just like there was no way she got to be in control. I gripped the back of her neck and kissed back, crushing my mouth to hers.

Kenzie's soft moan behind Bri, and Bri's grunt as she molded her body to mine were full on a fire I had no desire to extinguish.

This was about to get me in serious trouble.

Fuck yes.

FIFTEEN
BRIENNE

KISSING SCOTT WAS THE OPPOSITE OF KENZIE. SHE WAS sweetness and softness and safety.

He was hard, demanding, and dangerous in so many ways. When I was younger, bossy rich boys were for sex and walking away from to prove to them, to me, that I didn't need them for anything but their dicks. That wasn't what Scott was, as much as I might want to think that. He was compelling and creative and a kind of broken I understood at my core. The kind that faded but never vanished.

And he held my future in his hands in so many ways.

That didn't mean I was going to surrender anything to him.

He shifted the control of the kiss to back me into the wall near the closet. The move was enough for me to see Kenzie, watching with wide eyes and captivated. The accusation that had been there earlier was gone.

Scott pushed his tongue to dance with mine in my mouth. He gripped the back of my neck hard.

I wouldn't yield. I bit his bottom lip, and dug my fingers into his chest when I clenched his shirt in my fists.

His erection dug into my hip, and his body pinned me in place as he trailed his mouth down my jaw, to bite my neck.

My head was fuzzy, and I was drowning in this intensity. I shoved him back, needing room to breathe. I wouldn't give myself up. Not ever, especially not during sex. But it was so tempting now to shut my brain off completely. To keep feeling and stop thinking.

I couldn't.

"Is that a *no*?" Scott's question was ragged.

I wanted him. I was going to go out on a limb and assume he wanted me too. But I wanted them both. To be ravaged by Scott, to be saved by Kenzie.

There was no way I could walk away from whatever was happening here. I should, but I was in too deep. I had to know what came next. I had to find out how all of this played out, but it was going to be on my terms.

"It's a *not like this*." I slipped a finger along the waistband of my leggings. "But it's not a *no*."

I ignored my own reluctance to put any distance between us, and moved toward the couch again. I didn't want to fuck in their bed. Not tonight. I couldn't—

Before he was out of reach, I grabbed Scott and tugged him with me. For a moment he looked like he was going to protest. Exert control again.

It seemed like his curiosity won out, and he let me push him onto the couch.

Kenzie had moved with us, and I grasped her hands

as I sat on Scott's lap, my back to him. I pulled her between my legs and his for kisses, and let him steal her away to do the same before I slipped between them again and pressed my mouth to hers.

This let me feel them both. Let me keep Scott's lips on my neck. Not that I thought *no more mouth kisses* would change much, but it let me stay in control.

Kenzie knelt on the couch next to us, making it easier to keep her close and keep my mouth on hers. Except when Scott pushed between us to give her hungry kisses that heated me with their proximity. Their passion was tangible.

The feeling lingered when Kenzie came back to me. The warmth. The spark every time our lips met.

The angle of this was awkward to the point of being wrong, and I didn't care. Scott cupped my breasts and kneaded the ample flesh before slipping one hand between my legs to press into my core. To stroke and tease me through the leggings.

There was so much electricity surrounding all of us that I wanted to act without thinking. I wanted to *feel* everything. While I nibbled Kenzie's lips, I slid my hands down her chest. Into her shorts and under her panties. She was as wet as I had to be, and I wanted to bury myself in the slick warmth.

With hands and mouths roaming everywhere, my need crept higher. I slipped my fingers inside Kenzie, working in and out before gliding up to her clit. She gasped when I bumped the swollen button, and Scott's groan vibrated through my back.

Fuck. I circled her clit, watching the stunning expressions that flowed across her face. Captivated by her mounting pleasure. Her breath hitched and her body froze, and then she shuddered with climax when she came, grinding into me as she rode the sensation.

This wasn't enough. I wanted to feel Scott inside of me. But that would be—

No. I couldn't think about why that was or wasn't a good idea. When I stood, he reached for me, but I was faster.

Kenzie caught me though, fingers in my waistband. It was almost like magical Tetris. Kenzie pulled me back to her, while Scott molded his body to hers from behind. She yanked my pants down enough to expose me, and push her fingers between my legs.

The way Scott watched us, the hunger in his eyes, made me feel like I was being devoured without him ever touching me.

I half-lost myself in the sensation of Kenzie fingering me. Fucking me. Riding my clit as the pressure built inside me.

While she did, Scott tugged at her clothing. Unzipped his jeans. Penetrated her in a single thrust.

How the fuck was that so incredible to watch? Kenzie's growing sighs, Scott's grunts, were enough to coax my climax forward. I came hard, and I didn't want it to end. Even as the pleasure eased up, I needed more from her. I needed to keep kissing her. Keep tasting and playing with her.

I needed to make her come again while he was inside her.

I swallowed her cries when she did, and kept

pushing as Scott's movements stuttered, then flowed in at high impact. He was close too. He was spilling inside her. How much of the slickness on my fingers was her and what was him?

It didn't matter.

The frenzied feeling in the air slipped as we all slowed to a stop, but it didn't vanish. We all wilted into each other, catching our breath. Enjoying the afterglow.

There was enough discussion to agree we needed to be someplace more comfortable. We cleaned up and collapsed in their bed, Kenzie between Scott and me.

I was enjoying the fuck out of this. Scott was another complication I didn't need, and it was getting harder every day to ignore that I wanted them both. Over and over.

I was in so much trouble. My heart. My mind. My resolve.

So why couldn't I convince myself that doing this, that wanting them again, was a bad idea?

This wasn't just about sex anymore, and that scared me the most.

SIXTEEN
KENZIE

I LIKED HAVING SCOTT BACK. I LIKED WAKING UP NEXT
to Bri. It was twice as good finding myself between them
in the morning. I was glad we'd talked things out last
night.

"What's for breakfast?" Bri asked.

Imagine being bold enough to admit being hungry
first thing in the morning.

Imagine being so repressed that was a marvelous
thought. But the second one was already me, I didn't
need to imagine.

Scott grabbed his phone from the nightstand, and
rolled back into me immediately, to wrap an arm around
me while he scrolled. "You like croissants, Bri?"

"Literal croissants?" she asked.

Odd question. "As opposed to figurative ones?"

She sat up, her blanket falling away to leave her
exposed. She didn't make any move to cover herself
again. "As opposed to, I was looking for the innuendo in

the question and I couldn't find it. Maybe something about being buttery and flakey?"

"Maybe. If you figure it out, let me know." Scott jabbed at his screen. "In the meantime, I'm getting us sandwiches and coffee, unless there are any protests."

I shook my head. "None from me." This was easy. A smidge ridiculous. Natural.

"Until I figure out if there's a hidden message in your question, I'm in," Bri said.

Scott looked up from his phone long enough to give her a look of disbelief. "Why would there be innuendo or a hidden message in croissants?"

"I don't know. Sometimes people are weird." Bri shrugged.

"You're telling me." Scott chuckled and went back to ordering breakfast.

I couldn't remember why I'd freaked out last night.

Okay, I could a little. There were still hints of that shock and betrayal, but overall, this entire situation, listening to these two people banter, being in the middle of it—a part of it—felt right.

We dressed and kept up the random conversation until our food was delivered.

I was torn between the fun idea of all three of us on the couch, cuddling and sipping coffee, and the belief that breakfast should be eaten at the table, not in the living room. Propriety won out, and when the food showed up, I artfully guided us into the dining room, and laid out everyone's spots, with Bri across from Scott and me between them.

Okay, so maybe I wasn't one-hundred percent secure with this yet, but I was getting there.

We still needed to discuss Bri's *gift* from her grandfather. Or rather, how best to deal with it. "I hate to be the one to bring reality back into our lives, but how are you going to tell people at work?"

"Tell them what?" Scott asked.

Bri looked between him and me. "You mean about…?"

I should've clarified. "About the board seat." We also needed to have the other conversation, but that probably involved defining our relationship and there was such a thing as too much reality. I was in a good mood and wanted to stay here a bit longer.

"I doubt most people at work care," Bri said.

True. And I understood that because this was a privately held company, information really just needed to go to investors and be updated in the Articles of Incorporation. "I get that. But what about Chloe? Some of the other people in management?"

Scott groaned. "She's going to kill me."

"Why?" Bri asked. "You didn't make this decision, and I'm not quitting my job. First of all, I like my job. Second, a board seat doesn't pay anything. You still draw your income from somewhere else."

"Then make sure you tell her that, and that you do it in person." Problem solved. Not that it was really an issue, but it was one of those things that would bite back if it was ignored.

Scott reached across the table to nudge Bri. "Isn't she gorgeous when she's bossy?"

"It's pretty good, yeah." Bri gave me a polite nod. "Yes, mistress."

My cheeks heated, not just at the two of them ganging up with the compliment, but because I was helping. This decision was a little thing, but I liked being a part of it. A part of them.

"That can wait until Monday, though," Scott announced. "I'm not doing anything today except staying in and watching Godzilla movies."

That sounded like my kind of weekend.

"I *love* Godzilla movies." Bri's demeanor shifted to awe.

I grinned. "You are so going to fit in here."

"We do need to get your car," Scott said.

And Bri's, since I brought her here last night. "Drop me off at the diner, drop Bri off at the office. She can pack a bag for tonight and I can stop by the grocery store on the way home for the required snacks." Because movie day always required snacks.

"Like that, you're going to assume I want to stay the night?" Bri's tone was playful, but the challenge still made me stall.

"Yes. Like that." Scott didn't hesitate.

"So be it," Bri said.

An hour or so later, we were all at the condo again, with drinks staying cool in the fridge and chips and other assorted sweets and snacks waiting for us.

Our living room was set up so it really only took the push of a button, and the lighting shifted, along with the TV angle. It went from being a warm place to sit and talk, to a cozy place to lean back and watch movies.

As the morning turned to afternoon and then evening, we were talking more than we were watching the movies.

Bri returned from the kitchen with a fresh drink in hand, and I pulled her down between Scott and me, so I could lean against her. "Personal question," she said. "Are we at the point where I can stop prefacing those? Probably."

"We talked about our vaginas the morning after I met you." Did I just say that without thinking? It didn't matter that this was an intimate setting at home. I couldn't believe those words came out of my mouth.

"And I missed it?" Scott looked disappointed.

Bri rolled her eyes. "You've seen them both, and I'm sure you have your own distinct opinions."

Scott pursed his lips and furrowed his brow, then nodded as if this was the most serious thing he'd considered all day. "In that case, let's say we're past asking if questions are too personal."

"We'll see." Bri glanced over her shoulder at him. "Why don't you drink?"

Oh. This was *that* kind of personal.

"Why do you hate rich party boys?" Scott countered.

I had no idea how the questions were similar or why he'd assumed that.

Bri didn't look confused, though. She was almost smiling, but it was the kind of look that didn't reach her eyes. "Dad wanted a son to take over his legacy. When he got me, he tried to turn me into the kind of girl who would land him a son. He was willing to whore me out to anyone he deemed worthy. I learned to fuck them before they fucked me. I mean that both literally and figuratively. But I hated it."

Holy wow. She spoke with an iciness I didn't expect. What she was saying had to devour her, but there was no emotion in her voice.

"Your turn," Bri said.

"Dad wanted a son to take over his legacy. When he got me, he tried to turn me into the kind of boy who would make him proud. He was willing to whore me out to anyone who might make me a better man, and I learned to drink the pain away."

Christ, the two of them had been broken when they were younger. I knew that about Scott. I'd seen him deal with the after effects, and seeing the parallels to Bri...

When a smile cracked through on her face, I was surprised. Her look didn't break the somber mood, but it did lighten the mood a touch. She raised her root beer bottle over her shoulder, toward Scott. "To dads who fucks us up."

He clinked his can against her drink. "Fuck those guys."

They both took long swallows.

Bri focused on me. "It's okay."

"I don't— Why are you telling *me* that?" I didn't understand.

"You look worried. I've dealt with this, and I'm guessing Scott has too."

"But it hurt you both."

She nodded. "It did. And then we decided to stop letting it do so."

I was glad to hear it. I saw how the pain connected Bri and Scott, though. It was impossible to miss that bond between them that I'd never understand.

SEVENTEEN
SCOTT

I'D NEVER HATED MONDAYS. IN HIGH SCHOOL, THEY were my escape from home. By the time I graduated, Zach and I were already building Cord, our first company, and that meant I was going to a job made by me and for me. Double win.

But some Mondays, I was more reluctant to leave home behind. The weekend had been incredible— Kenzie was happy, I was having fun, and Bri was at least partly to thank for both of those things.

The thought of behaving around her at work was more than mildly disappointing, but I supposed I could suck it up for now.

We scheduled a meeting with Chloe, to get the *big* news out of the way. Not that it was any sort of news at all. Our board of directors had so little say in day-to-day work, and for the most part we agreed with each other. Still, the position did give Bri a certain level of power. It changed the dynamic.

When I walked into Chloe's office, Bri was already

there. The tiny smile that passed her face wouldn't mean anything to most people, but it spoke volumes to me. A quiet reminder of what we'd shared over the last few days.

Chloe listened quietly while we explained the situation about Bri taking over her grandfather's board seat. Pursed her lips and nodded when Bri said, "I still work for you, though. I'm still your assistant."

"But it's not the same, is it." *There* was Chloe's protest. "You have control over my job now. You can decide tomorrow I pissed you off, and that's that."

"No single board member has that kind of say over anyone's job. That's why you're all here." I could phrase it more diplomatically, but this was the truth. Each of my VP's was the best at what they did, and they were each vocal and stubborn enough to piss people off on occasion.

Chloe let out a sound that was half-scoff, half bark. "That worked out really well for Jordan."

Great to see she wasn't still bitter about that. Though, I wasn't happy with how any of that had gone either. "That was a legal issue, and once it was cleared up, he chose not to come back."

"I know." Chloe huffed a sign.

"I want to keep working for you," Bri said. "I choose that. Are we okay?"

Chloe seemed to consider the question for a moment. "Yeah, we're good." She extended her hand to Bri. "Congratulations, by the way. There are a lot of assholes out there, and you're not one of them. You'll be good in this spot."

That was more like it.

"Thank you." Bri shook Chloe's hand.

Easy peasy. I stood and clapped. "No more questions? We're good? Good. Back to work."

"Actually, Scott, I need just a few minutes of your time." Chloe's request didn't surprise me, she could want to talk about anything.

Why did I think this might be a sensitive subject?

"Would you grab me a coffee, Bri?" Chloe asked.

Yup. This was about to get interesting.

Bri agreed, and I made sure not to stare too long as she walked out of the room, and closed the door behind her.

"What's up?" I turned back to Chloe.

"I remember when you guys brought Kenzie in. For PR."

Fuck. "Okay. Cool."

"I remember you're real shitty at keeping secrets."

"No clue what you're talking about." Bullshit. I knew exactly what she was talking about. I really hadn't hidden at all that Kenzie and I were fucking back then. Why keep it a secret?

Chloe drummed her fingers on her desk and watched them move, rather than looking at me. "I'm grateful for the rules we have about dating—lack of rules, whatever."

Yeah, this could get awkward. I'd rather have any version of this conversation with her than with most people. Chloe had a boyfriend and a girlfriend. She wasn't likely to give me some sort of lecture about *this could destroy your home life*.

That didn't mean I wanted to talk about if anything was going on with Bri. Especially not before I defined that for myself. "You have a point, get to it."

Chloe and I had known each other since she was a kid. Her sister was Zach's wife, and one of my best friends. Chloe had never held back with me, even when she was ten and telling me I was a stupid, smelly boy.

"My point is, do *not* fuck this up for Bri," Chloe said. "Whatever's going on, whatever you think it is you want or need. I'm going to assume, because I know you, that Kenzie knows, but do not damage Bri's future with this."

I wanted to ask how Chloe could tell. How much she'd figured out. What she'd noticed, so I could hide it. Not that I'd stop, though. "I won't. Not that I know what you're talking about."

She raised her eyebrows. "Okay. Good."

The next few hours were a blur of catching up on anything that came in over the weekend, and prepping for SXSW—the show we were announcing our new Nashville venture at. At eleven, I stepped into the Monday morning touch base with upper management.

Our assistants took turns taking notes in these things, and I was happier than maybe I should be that it was Bri's week. We let everyone know about her new position on the board, and a wave of *congratulations* and *condolences* floated around the room.

If anyone had any issues with it, there would be more private meetings in my future, but it seemed as though no one else was batting an eye. I hoped when the news reached anyone else who understood it, that things continued to go this smoothly for her.

This was a meeting for details; it was all high-level check-in. What were their teams working on, who needed more people or time or money. Today was no different, with one exception. Any time someone mentioned changes—wanting to grow, updating policy, adding new tools, anything that might need higher up approval depending on cost—they glanced at Bri.

Every. Fucking. Time.

"We have the building and location estimates for the new call center. I'll send that up so you can pass it along." Judith glanced at Bri then back at her laptop screen.

"Stop." I wasn't doing this. If we cleared things up now, then we could get back to business. "Bri's not going to be the reason you stop getting budget for anything. Nothing has changed since last Friday."

"He's right. You all know better than that." Zach backed me up.

"But is it really all the same?" Chloe asked.

A shadow crossed Bri's face. "Yes. I want the same thing we all want, for the same reasons."

"Which are?" It was unlikely Elliot was being mean. More likely cautious.

Still, it set me on edge. If they were struggling with this thing that wasn't supposed to matter, others would too. I wanted to answer for Bri, but that wouldn't help.

Not that she needed anyone to step in. She sat straighter in her chair and looked him in the eye. "I want us to succeed because I like what we do, and I like what *I* do. I don't know your jobs any better than you know mine, and I'm not going to use this as an excuse to destroy what obviously works."

That seemed to be the answer they needed, and the meeting rapidly returned to what it should be.

We were wrapping up when lunch came. That signaled the end of the meeting, and that we got to hang out and bullshit for the next little while.

"Bri, I understand you found Elliot's secret science experiment," Judith said between bites of burger.

Bri picked a cucumber off her salad and nibbled. "Is it really a secret if it's on a test machine in an unlocked office?"

"Everything's an open secret in this company. Never think it's not." Chloe glanced at me.

Apparently we weren't all good.

If anyone else noticed, they didn't so much as flinch.

"In that case, I did find it. Is it new game content?" Bri asked.

"Absolutely not." Zach looked grossly dissatisfied with his own salad. Not that I blamed him. We weren't even forty—it hardly seemed fair that he had to worry about stupid things like high blood pressure and heart attacks.

"It could be new game content." No surprise that Elliot was pushing this.

Chloe gave a brief shake of her head. "It could be a PR nightmare, you mean."

"Since when is that an issue?" Judith asked.

Chloe rolled her eyes. "Since nudity."

Not *ever* a problem for her. We'd hired her, years ago, because she wrote some of the best fan fiction of our characters that there was. Explicit, sexy, rated X fanfiction, but it was still a quality story.

"There are limits." Good ol' Zach. Always the voice of reason.

Sometimes I hated that.

"I thought they looked good," Bri said. "We make games for adults anyway. People don't know our characters are naked under their clothes?"

Elliot pushed his food aside. He was getting serious. "But they're not. There are more pixels under there, not real junk."

"Are you for it or against it?" Bri looked confused.

He was totally for it. This was his way of justifying the content to censors.

"The only way to do it is a new game." As I reiterated, that rush was back. This time louder. More distinct. *Okay.*

"Okay," Elliot said.

Judith nodded. "Let's make it happen."

Okay. My brain was louder this time. *New game. New toys. New discoveries. New fun.*

"Not under Rinslet's name you can't." Zach. Keeper of the rules.

Judith smirked. "Let's bring it to the board."

"Picture it now." Elliot slipped into a deeper, more announcer-style voice. "A game made for actual adults that has actual adult content. Not slaughter and death, but sex. Weird, right? Make people admit sex is a thing?"

"No," Zach repeated.

Damn it, damn it, damn it. "Fuck. I hate to say this,

but he's right." Except that the phrase *new game* was stuck in my head. It wasn't Elliot's pitch making me want to do this, it was the challenge that would go with the new project.

Fucking hell I wanted this, and I hated that Zach was right. Maybe ten years ago, when we didn't have a multi-billion dollar company riding on decisions like this.

When did I become part of a machine I didn't control?

We wrapped up lunch, and everyone headed back to their desks. It was Bri's job to clean up, and she shooed me out when I offered to help.

"Scott." Her voice stopped me as I reached the door.

I did like the way my name sounded rolling off her lips. "Hmm?"

"What's stopping you from telling them yes?"

"So many things."

"Are any of them things you can't work around? There's always a solution, right?" Bri said. "I'd play a game like that."

I couldn't answer her because there wasn't a solution and I so desperately wanted there to be one.

EIGHTEEN
BRIENNE

Tuesday around lunch, Reception called up to say my dad was at the Rinslet offices to see me.

I didn't want to talk to him, but I wasn't going to leave the front desk to clean up my mess, either. I took the elevator down and found him waiting in the lobby.

He greeted me with a quick hug and a kiss on the cheek—something he hadn't done since I lived at home.

I wasn't subtle about pulling away. "What do you want?"

A small group of people walked in behind me, and I heard the whispers. "Is that Chester Jr.?"

I hid my wince. So much for keeping who I was a secret?

"I'm here to talk about my father's call the other day," Dad said. "I wanted to make sure you'd hear me out."

In other words, he thought he'd come to my place of employment and try to shame me into talking to him, because he knew I wouldn't take his calls. "I'm not interested."

"Be reasonable, Brienne. You've been handed a huge responsibility, and I'm here to ensure you have the resources you need."

Wow. He was really doing this here.

A pair of developers walked by, crossing from the elevator to the exit, saying something about the project in Nashville, and the game security engine. How awesome things were looking for the show in Austin.

"I have what I need to take care of things, thank you." I moved toward the exit, expecting him to fall into step with me.

He didn't budge, and I was forced to face him again.

"You say that." His voice was disconcertingly calm. "But you've never been on a board of directors before. And for your first time to be when you have a job at a company where you're only an assistant?" His voice carried, and his disdain for my job was palpable.

More of my co-workers glanced in our direction.

It figured he chose to do this around noon, while so many people were coming and going from lunch.

"I know this company and its policies enough to help direct them. I've got it under control." I wouldn't let him see me falter, but I did spare a glance at Reception, and hoped my look conveyed *help*. "I'd like you to leave now."

Another group of developers walked by, talking about Austin again.

"I'll leave when we're done talking." Dad's tone was infuriatingly smooth. "You look like you're on edge.

Should we go sit in the cafeteria? I could buy you lunch. You don't look like you're eating."

I didn't remember a time when my father was concerned about my weight being too low. When I was a teenager, one of his favorite reminders was that if I had that next piece of cheese, that was one more boy who would be turned off by my chubby thighs. "I'm fine, thank you," I said.

"I'm glad to hear it."

I doubted that, but the longer we stood here, the more people stopped and stared. I couldn't be rude to him, in this place I actually cared about, where people only saw this conversation. Where they had no idea how he'd treated me in the past. I'd been through that kind of judgment before, and I didn't need it coloring what my colleagues thought of me.

"What else do you want to talk about?" I asked.

"*Chester.*" Scott's voice boomed through the lobby, carrying over everything else.

Relief rushed through me, fueled by a shiver of delight that he'd come to my rescue. I shouldn't care, but I did.

"It's been a long time." Scott crossed the lobby quickly to join us.

My father's smile shifted in a blink, from controlling to pleasant. "Scott. How've you been? I've been hoping to get on your calendar."

"So I've heard." Scott ignored Dad's outstretched hand, though he was definitely within handshaking distance. "Leave now." His voice dropped to a more threatening tone. "Or I'll have you arrested for trespassing."

Dad's mask cracked. "Excuse me?"

One of the building security officers joined us.

"This is Reggie." Scott nodded at the new arrival. "He'll ensure you make it off the premises successfully."

I was positively giddy at my father's fury as he was escorted from the building.

"Come on," Scott barked to a room full of gawking people. "You all have jobs to do. Back to it." He gestured toward the elevator bank.

"Let's go back upstairs," he said more softly to me. We stepped into a waiting car that was gratefully empty. "Are you all right?" Like that, his tone shifted toward concern.

My heart did a little flippy move. "I'm okay, thank you." I wasn't some damsel in distress who needed the big bad boss to come to her rescue.

That didn't stop me from liking that he cared. Then again, he might've done that for anyone.

Sure. The head of the company would've personally sought out any employee having issues with a visitor, and seen to it himself that they left the building.

"Good." Scott's smile made my insides gooey. We were in a public space. Anyone could join us on any floor. The lift rested at my stop. "Be safe." The look he gave me felt deeper than it should. Like if he held my gaze long enough, he could see into my soul.

I shook the avalanche of thoughts aside. "Thank you."

I stepped from the elevator and went back to work.

A few hours later, I walked into a meeting, and the entire room went silent. I swore every eye in the place was on me. "Do I have something on my face? Is my skirt stuck in my panties?" I joked.

I got a few nervous laughs in return, and things returned to normal. Kind of weird.

At the end of the day, I refused to let myself call Kenzie to see if she was busy. This wasn't that kind of relationship, and I was already getting too close. Time to sever those ties and step back to life as it had been.

Tuesday, I heard the whispers. The ones with my name and the furtive glances in my direction. The ones that talked about who my father was, who my grandfather was, what I had become to the company. Every meeting I walked into, a large part of the room went silent when they saw me.

Kenzie messaged me that afternoon. *Are you free after work?*

I knew for a fact that Scott wasn't, because I'd scheduled the planning meetings with him and Chloe. The only reason Kenzie wanted my company was because she couldn't have his.

Knowing that, why was it so hard to reply and say *I have plans?*

By Wednesday, it was clear most everyone knew who I was and what my new position was with the company. People who were normally friendly became cold. Most of my interactions were either overly polite or came with barely masked hostility, and it all sucked.

Scott sent me a note over messenger. *We're watching Mothra save Japan tonight. Want to help us cheer?*

I *wanted* life to go back to the way it was three weeks ago. Would I give up the memories and the time with Kenzie and Scott for that?

I refused to let myself consider the answer to my own question.

Thursday night I stayed late at work. It was easier to get a lot of things done without looking up and seeing someone staring—sneering—at me. Staying at the office also meant not going home alone. Something I'd *never* had a problem with before. When I was younger, *alone* was salvation.

It was almost seven at night when my messenger pinged. I pushed back the flutters in my chest at Scott's name.

Scott: You still here?

I could ignore him. Pretend I didn't see the message or that I'd left my messenger online when I was away.

Me: Yes.

Scott: Busy?

Me: Presumably.

Scott: Come upstairs. I need your help scheduling travel.

Bullshit. That was the easy answer. *I'm busy.*

Even if I was in the habit of telling the executives I didn't have time for them, I wanted to see him outside of a meeting setting. I wanted to talk to him without wondering who was watching and what kind of gossip they were spreading.

Me: Be right there.

The building was a ghost town. Usually when I was here late, so were a lot of other people. It meant crunch time. All hands on deck. Tonight, most of the lights were out, and the only sound was the hum of electricity.

I walked into Scott's office and closed the door behind me without thought.

Why did I do that?

His grin when he saw me was bright. Warm. "Hey."

"Hey. You needed help scheduling travel?" I wasn't going to lose my cool. Nope. Not in any way.

"Yeah. Ivan usually takes care of this for me, and I can't figure it out."

"Bullshit."

Scott's eyes grew wide, but his amusement didn't fade. "Excuse me?"

"You're going to tell me the brains behind the technology in this company, *the* man who came up with whatever makes people use those buzzwords when they talk about us, is incapable of figuring out how to book his own flight?"

Scott shrugged and sank back in his seat. "Busted. But it got you up here, didn't it?"

"You could've just said *I want to see you.*" This was where I should leave.

"Would you have come up here in that case?" He

had a good point. "Besides, messenger leaves a paper trail. This is plausible deniability."

I turned away. "Great. I'm heading out."

Scott grabbed my wrist. How did he move so fast? He turned me to face him again, but now he was closer. His hand was still on my arm.

My brain stalled.

"I do want your thoughts on something." The playfulness was gone from his voice.

I needed this to not be serious. "I'm not going to tell you if your dick looks bigger here than it does at home."

He chuckled. "Not that. Please?"

"I'm listening." I pulled from his grasp and crossed my arms.

He leaned his weight against his desk, half-sitting. It didn't put much distance between us, but it was enough for me to breathe again.

"It's this memoir book contract," he said. "I owe them an answer, and I need honest input from someone who probably understands where I'm coming from."

The vulnerability caught me off-guard. How hard was it for him to admit he needed this kind of help?

"Talk to me." I made myself comfortable in the seat across from him.

"Would you like to hear a story only a very small number of people know?"

"I hope you don't expect me to say *no* to that. Is this a secret? Something just between us?"

Scott rested his hands on the desk, pressing down hard enough that his skin paled around the creases where the edge of the wood dug into his palms. "It's not something those of us involved hide so much as it's just something we don't talk about. Should I be worried I'm going to see you on Jenquiry tomorrow morning, spilling my guts?"

No. Spreading stories to the wrong people was a terrible thing, regardless of how true the stories were. "Jen doesn't really do gossip. There is this new girl though... Fallyn?"

"Breaks games. Picks on Elliot. Not worried about her."

We were dancing around the subject. "If you don't want to tell me, you don't have to." I'd hate for someone to make me bare my soul, and I certainly wasn't going to do it to him.

Scott puffed out his cheeks and they deflated with his long exhale. "About thirty-eight years ago, there was a couple. High school sweethearts. He was the quarterback, she was the head cheerleader and they both came from wealthy families. Think *perfect 80's popular couple—* that was them."

"I don't watch a lot of 80's movies, but from what I know, those couples were rarely the ones who got their happily ever after." The story had my attention, though.

"I said what I said. In fact, this couple *broke up* right before their senior prom. He didn't like her being nice to another football player, she called him a possessive asshole... I'm sure the entire thing was messy and angsty."

His tone was almost detached. This wasn't one of those humor-filled stories I'd heard him tell in other settings.

Scott pushed away from the desk and paced the span of the office. "To prove to his cheerleader that he didn't need her, the quarterback took someone else to prom. Woman number two was the poor girl in their class. The shy, bookish one. Supposedly, she was thrilled to have a big jock show an interest in her.

I knew what that was like, as much as I hated to admit it. When I was that age, I was desperate for the right person to pay attention to me, just so I could fucking fit in. For even a moment. Rebelling was all well and good, but there were days that I'd been so lonely.

Though I didn't seek that kind of validation anymore, the memories stung. I assumed this story was about Scott's parents, given the timeframe and the way he was trying to stay detached, but there was more to it. I just hadn't figured out what yet.

"He fucked the shy girl on prom night. That oughta show that cheerleader, right?" Scott didn't pause in his pacing. If anything, his movement became more pronounced. "Probably lied about wearing protection. Dumped her the next day and less than a week after that, was boning the cheerleader again. They all went back to being them. The cheerleader girlfriend got pregnant, but she was able to hide until after graduation, and he had an heir to the family car dealership line he was about to take over."

This was definitely Scott's story. What was the twist?

"Fast-forward eighteen years to the day my mother decided she'd had enough of my father, and she walked out on him. That was the same day I found out he'd gotten his prom date pregnant too."

"Oh." I maybe should've seen that coming.

"You put all the pieces together yet?"

I didn't have enough information. What was I missing? "No."

"I didn't either. Not until she told me. Even though my best friend was only a few weeks older than me. Even though he'd been in my life for as long as I could remember, the poor kid who shouldn't have been at the rich kid schools, who my mom treated as she did me. She had to spell it out for me that Zach was my half-brother."

Oh. I didn't have anything to say about that, but I couldn't keep my surprise from my face.

Scott scrubbed his face. "His mom never wanted anything to do with my dad after that night. She asked for one thing—that her son be able to go to college. He had a trust fund we didn't know about, in exchange for his mother's silence. My mom hated the entire thing, but never him and never his mother."

His smirk didn't reach his eyes. "So our big *fuck you* to Dad was to take our college funds and start Cord."

"Wow." I was still speechless. "That's one hell of an origin story."

"That's why I don't know if I should write this memoir. How do I tell a story about the software empire that started as Cord, that broke and rose again from the ashes as Rinslet, without bringing his mom's and my mom's names into things? Fuck Dad, but Mom? All the others who have been hurt along the way?

"A lot of people will tell you I don't care what the public thinks, but that's only true when it comes to me. I try to live a *do no harm* kind of life, and these stories could definitely do harm."

"Sometimes that can't be helped." I understood his dilemma. Would I fare any better if the decision was mine? Unlikely.

"This time it can be," he said.

Easy enough. "Then don't sign the contract."

"But I like telling stories. I want to tell this story, and I know given everything I just said, that makes me sound selfish."

"Then I don't know what to tell you."

Scott paused long enough to search my face. "What would you do in my shoes?"

Nope. I wasn't taking that responsibility on. "My mother walked out shortly after I was born. She got fed up with Dad way before the eighteen year mark, and left me with him. I don't have the same quandary you do."

"I'm sorry."

"Me too."

Scott moved back to his spot on my side of the desk, and pulled me to my feet as he half-sat on the wood. "I need you at eye level. I need to know you're my equal in this conversation."

"In any conversation."

"True." He almost smiled.

This traipse into the past was sinking into my head. "Why do they do this to us? Why did we have to be vessels for someone else's ambitions?"

"Some people are driven."

Lousy excuse. "*You're* driven. You don't use the

people around you that way, or you and I wouldn't be talking."

"And some people see the rest of the world as pawns. Objects to be moved and placed—especially the objects they help create." He hadn't let go of my hands, and he rubbed his thumbs across the backs of my knuckles.

"That's a cold thought." Not that I would describe it any other way. "And out of it comes a broken fucked up little girl and a broken fucked up little boy." The words stung, because they were real. They reminded me of those times when I thought less of myself, and that there were still moments when I didn't believe I deserved love.

It also reminded me why getting close to Scott or Kenzie or anyone was a terrifying idea.

Scott widened his stance enough to pull me between his legs, and I didn't resist. I wanted to feel this connection. He squeezed my fingers. "When the Japanese mend broken cups—"

"They fill the cracks with gold and it's beautiful." I finished the thought for him. "I have the internet and I've seen the memes. Don't give me this *your scars are pretty* bullshit."

He glided his hands up my arms, pausing at my neck to trace the ink that decorated my throat. "To be far, a lot of your scars are stunning."

"I have a good tattoo artist." Was I changing the subject? Was he? Either way, I didn't want to dwell in the pain.

"The thing is, you didn't become *him*. You didn't let his influence do that to you," Scott said.

"And you didn't either," I countered. "Your mother

made sure you and your brother had something else. Could be something else. Maybe she's okay with you telling this story."

"Maybe."

"You could ask her. But I'm sure you've already done that."

Scott's smile grew a hint more. "I could probably ask her. Maybe you could ask yourself if it's okay to forgive you."

That didn't make any sense.

Or did it? What was I missing out on by using my past as a shield? For instance, was I giving up the chance to keep two incredible people in my life?

Scott cupped my face between his palms to look me in the eye. "Broken or not, I'm glad you're here," he said.

The way he was watching me made my heart skip. If he kissed me, I wouldn't push him away like I did the other night. I wouldn't have Kenzie to redirect him to.

The door behind me clicked open, and my stomach sank.

"I see nothing. I know nothing." That was Elliot.

The door closed again.

Fuck. What now?

"Oops." Scott let out a light chuckle.

It was as if the sound shattered the heavy cloud engulfing us, and I laughed. He joined in, though this wasn't funny at all. After a moment or two, we caught ourselves.

He pressed his forehead to mine. "I'll talk to him. Anyone else, I might be worried. Him? We'll be fine."

"Feel better about this memoir thing?" It was nearly impossible for me to go back to real conversation, when all I wanted to do was sink further into Scott.

"Getting there, thank you. Do me a few favors?"

"Depends, but try me."

"If you miss Kenzie as much as she does you, call her. See if she wants to hang out this weekend." Scott tilted his head closer, pressing his lips to my ear. "And lock the door behind you next time we're alone in a room together."

"You got it, boss." I was making a mistake by giving in. To both of them. But maybe it was safe for me to start healing.

NINETEEN
KENZIE

I TOLD MYSELF BRI HAD JUST BEEN BUSY, BUT THERE WAS a nagging doubt that I hadn't heard from her for a more severe reason. What if she saw this relationship differently than I did? What if it was nothing to her? When she called and invited me to a renaissance fair, I couldn't ignore my giddy excitement.

"I don't have anything to wear." Once upon a time that had been a stress for me. It took maneuvering to attend certain parties, for clients, for my career, because I couldn't afford another dress that was appropriate for whatever event. It was odd to be saying that again now, for very different reasons.

Fortunately, Bri was ready with a solution. "I'll hook you up. Meet me at the park Saturday and I'll make sure you're covered." She gave me an address and some instructions on how to find the place.

"I'll be there."

I got to the address in question far too early on the day of the fair—Faire according to the banner they were currently hanging at one of the park entrances. Bri wasn't here yet. Half the set-up crew wasn't here. I killed as much time as was possible circling the location.

Should I stop for coffee? Was that allowed at an event like this? Paper cups probably weren't very period specific. Why was I overthinking everything? I hadn't been this bad in years.

But I really wanted to do things right with Bri.

When I decided I'd wasted enough time to not be there unfashionably early, I pulled into the parking lot, and was relieved when Bri arrived a few moments later.

"Morning." I gave her a bright smile.

"Hey. I'm glad you came." She pulled me in for a quick peck on the lips.

Were we doing that now? There was no one here, so it wasn't as though a crowd had witnessed it. How public was I willing to be about this undefined thing?

"Come on. I'll introduce you to Manda. She's got our dresses." Bri grabbed my hand and led me toward the tents.

I loved the way her palm nestled against mine and that she knew exactly where we were going and what we were doing. We wove through people bringing in hand-carts and very modern wagons loaded with all sorts of goods.

Exciting.

Bri led us toward a tent near one end of a long row of them, with a weathered wooden stall out front. "Knock knock," she called as we drew closer.

"Back here," a disembodied voice replied.

Bri lifted the flap on the tent and let us in. Inside was

lit by two strings of LEDs hanging in an X along the ceiling.

"Are those period-appropriate?" Was I allowed to ask that?

The woman in the middle of it all wore a brown and green dress cinched around the torso with a corset. The dozens of thin pink braids that were her hair trailing down her back made a stark contrast to her clothing.

"Aye, Lass. Enchanted by a wizard they were." Her accent was wobbly at best. "And if anyone else asks, that's what you tell them." She slipped into a more local tone. "So happy you made it." She threw her arms around Bri.

The women hugged tightly, and Bri stepped back. "Manda, this is Kenzie. Kenzie, this is my ride-or-die BFF until eternity."

"Nice to meet you." I extended my hand. Was I supposed to curtsy or something? How in character did we need to be?

Manda looked between me and Bri. "Is this her? In the flesh?"

Bri nodded.

"Who am I?" Wow, that hit differently than I expected it to.

Manda gave me a quick hug. "The woman stealing Bri's heart."

"Manda." There was a warning in Bri's voice, and she received a shrug in return.

"I promise I don't gossip," Manda said to me. "So whatever you are, whomever you are, I'm not going to tell anyone. Just swear to me you're being nice to my Brienne."

I liked her. "I think she's doing more for me than the other way around. She really is the best."

Bri's smile was softer, shyer, than I was used to. And it was gorgeous.

"I have to set up." Manda stepped toward the tent flaps. "Dresses are over there, so go ahead and change." She gestured to a hook on the opposite side of the space —all of four or five feet away. "There are no locks on ye olde doors here, but this is my tent, no one is coming in but me, so I promise you won't get peeped on."

"Thank you." Bri squeezed her friend's hand and Manda left.

Bri didn't hesitate to strip out of her clothing, fold it up, and set it on a nearby table. She pulled on a dress that was more like a floor length nightgown as-is, then grabbed a corset and fitted it around her waist.

She turned her back to me. "Tie me up?"

"Umm… Here? Now?" I kept my tone playful, despite the pictures dancing in my head of one or the other of us being tied up. Played with.

Bri laughed. "Not like that. Filing the idea away for later though."

Yummy. I let heat and amusement flit through me as I stepped behind her to do up her laces. This close, the faintest scent of peaches teased me, and her soft skin reminded me how much fun it was to kiss her. To do more with her.

I leaned in and pressed a soft kiss to her back, below her neck. Was that okay?

Her soft sigh said *yes*. I lay a steady row of them down along her neck and shoulders as I finished tightening her bodice.

"Now you." Bri turned to face me.

I wasn't as bold about stripping down to my undies as she had been, despite her having seen me in less. It took conscious thought not to hide myself behind something, but I did like the look in her eyes as she watched me, open and unabashed.

"When we're done here today, we should find someplace less public to help each other out of our dresses," she said.

I liked that kind of playful promise. "Deal."

When she tied my corset into place, she treated me to a delicious string of kisses and nibbles along my skin.

This was the kind of fun that made me reluctant to leave the tent and join the real world.

I'd always wanted to see a real Ren Faire though, and I wasn't going to miss the chance.

Outside the tent, we stopped at Manda's booth first. She had shelves of handmade jewelry that sparkled in the morning sunshine. She wore a frown that hadn't been there when she left us.

"Are you all right?" Bri asked.

Manda wiped a hand over her face, but the smile that appeared didn't reach her eyes. "It's that thing I told you about. The zoning."

Words I knew. "Can I help?"

"Probably not, but thank you."

"She actually probably can," Bri said. "She got me

in to see Grandpa. She's a bad ass boss bitch with the phone calls."

I didn't know if I'd go that far, but that was one hell of a title to put on a business card. "What's going on?"

"We're growing." Manda gestured broadly. "We need a bigger space, and those of us that run the event found a bigger one. One that has an opening once a month so we can do this as long as weather permits. But some of the paperwork, the requests for zoning…" She scrunched her face up. "None of us knows quite enough to wade through the legalese. We can't afford a lawyer. We don't want to fuck things up."

"I can help with a lot of that." Not that I could offer law advice, but I'd seen my share of contracts, and I knew who to call for a large number of zoning and permit questions and issues.

"I can't ask you to—"

Bri smacked Manda lightly. "You didn't ask, she offered. Come on. This is your chance to get huge."

"I'd really love to help." As I said the words it hit me how much I meant them. This was my jam. I could make this right for her.

Manda twisted her mouth this way and that. "Okay. That would be awesome. I don't have the stuff on me, but could I call you?"

"Any time. I swear, I'm not a busy person." I gave her my number.

We browsed her jewelry, and I found the perfect bracelet. Blue crystals set in a delicate bronze chain. The entire thing glittered and sparkled in the sunlight as I twisted and turned my wrist.

Manda tried to give it to me for free, but I insisted this was her business and I had to pay like any customer.

"Where to now?" Bri asked as we strolled away.

I had no idea. There was so much to see. "What do you usually do?"

"Vendors first. Food and games after. Then vendors again."

"It sounds like a plan."

Bri grabbed my hand and tugged me toward a booth with leather accessories.

I wanted to enjoy the casual moment, but my traitor of a brain reminded me we were in public. I was holding another woman's hand in front of a lot of other people, some of whom may know me. Was I ready to tell the world I was seeing someone?

Why didn't I think about this before?

The rational part of my brain argued that what Bri was doing right now, guiding me to a new spot, wasn't taboo or unusual. Friends did things like this. And even if it meant more to me, maybe I needed to chill the fuck out.

The mental fight consumed my mind in a way I didn't care for, and when we stopped at the next booth, I tried to be polite about dropping Bri's hand as quickly as possible.

She gave me a glance and a curious look, but turned back to a pair of leather bracelets hanging from a wooden pegged tree full of them.

The next few hours were a blur of new and fun, and I would've enjoyed it all a lot more if my brain didn't spend most of the time asking if I was acting the way I should be with Bri. We couldn't be a couple in public, but I'd missed her. I didn't want to miss out on the little intimate touches.

A man with a camera stopped us on our way to a sword swallowing show.

"A photographer? Here?" I didn't realize that would be a thing.

"'Tis not a modern camera, m'lady, 'tis a magical image capture device," he said.

Bri laughed. "Granted its powers by a great wizard?"

"Exactly. A powerful and kind wizard who wishes the realm to remember the fun to be had today." The cameraman spoke with flourish.

That was fun.

"We're in." Bri pulled me close for a pose. As she leaned closer, I realized she was about to kiss me. Full on the lips.

Time slowed to a crawl. I turned my head at the last second, and her lips landed on my cheek.

The world seemed to freeze until the cameraman handed us a card. "You can check the magical words out in the tent by the exit. Enjoy the rest of the day."

Bri was staring at me, and I didn't know what to say.

"We need to talk, don't we?" She asked.

Probably.

"Kenzie." A familiar voice reached us and pierced my thoughts. My smile slipped into place on instinct, and we turned to see Barb and another woman from the charity circuit approaching us. "It is you." Barb grinned.

She and the other woman wore elegant velvet

dresses with heavy ornamentation, that made our little frocks feel like peasant outfits.

"What are you doing here?" I tried to silence the negative part of my brain. The panicking part.

"We're just checking out this adorable little thing. Wouldn't it be fun to do some sort of fundraising like this?" Barb asked.

So much fun.

"Who's your friend?" Barb kept talking as if I was keeping up my half of the conversation.

My brain froze. What was I supposed to say? "This is Bri. She's showing me around."

"How do you know each other?" The other woman —I couldn't remember her name, I was so mind locked —asked.

Bri opened her mouth.

"She works for one of the executives at Scott's company." I heard the words tumble past my lips, and I couldn't stop them. "I mean, she's a friend, obviously. She's—"

"Just someone who works at her husband's office." Bri's tone cooled. "That's it."

"No. That's not it." Fuck me. *Make this right.*

Bri looked sugary sweet. "It is. That's all it is. Showing the boss's wife how the rest of us live."

"So fun. We'll see you around." Barb and her friend waved and wandered away.

Bri turned away too and stalked in another direction.

I hurried to catch up to her. "Wait, please."

"Show starts soon." Her voice was cold.

"Please, Bri. Talk to me."

"You don't want that."

I really did, though.

We sat through sword swallowing and a show with whips that was as much humor as skill. I didn't see most of it. I kept fumbling for words. Every time I opened my mouth, Bri would silence me with a look.

As we walked out of the clearing used as an amphitheater, Scott approached us. "We wrapped up early." He wrapped an arm around my waist, and pressed his lips to mine in a long kiss. "What did I miss?"

"I need to go." Bri took a step back. "Give the dress back to Manda when you're done." She strode off, ignoring all of my pleas for her to wait.

"What did I miss?" Scott asked again, his voice tighter this time.

I'd fucked up. So so badly. "I don't know what to do."

TWENTY

BRIENNE

T<small>HIS WAS A MISTAKE.</small>

This was a mistake.

This was a mistake.

The short song taunted me the entire drive back to my apartment.

The chorus was *She works for one of Scott's executives.*

It was a horrible tune. Worst music I'd heard this year.

And I couldn't get it out of my head.

By the time I got home, tears of frustration pricked my eyelids. I refused to cry over these people. They weren't worth it.

I stalked into my apartment, and slammed the door behind me. It didn't make me feel better the way I hoped, especially when the neighbor's dog started barking in response, and my dress got stuck between the door and the frame.

I yanked the fabric free and fumbled to get out of the clothes as quickly as possible. The strings on the corset were out of reach. This wasn't made to be taken off alone. Letting out a muffled growl of frustration, I twisted the restrictive clothing around.

A ripping sound reached my ears, tears almost spilled over.

No crying. This didn't get sadness.

I managed to get out of the dress and tossed it on the couch. Manda tried to warn me, and I should've listened. Couples were always a bad idea.

I was so sure I was in control. That I could stay removed, and then I made a mistake and let Kenzie and Scott in.

It didn't feel like a mistake at the time.

Kenzie wanted to talk. To apologize. But she made so many assumptions. It had been easier to assume than to talk when she saw me this morning.

I thought we'd gotten good at talking. That had been as much fun as the sex.

I could've initiated the conversation as easily as she could.

Not the point.

And that stupid song was still stuck in my head.

This was a mistake.

She works for one of Scott's executives.

Kenzie's default hadn't even been *this is my girlfriend.* She had to remove me from herself by at least two degrees.

She tried to correct it. *This is my friend.* That was fair. Even *She works for Scott* would've been better, though it still would have pissed me off.

Unforgivable.

I pulled on the biggest, most oversized sweatshirt I

owned, along with a baggy pair of sweats, and curled up on my couch under a knit throw. I sent Manda a text.

> Me: I accidentally tore one of your corsets. I'm sorry.

Manda: Where did you go?

Manda: What happened?

Manda: Kenzie said you left.

> Me: She didn't tell you why?

Manda: She said she fucked up.

I couldn't imagine Kenzie using the word *fuck*.

> Me: That about covers it.

Manda: Tell me what happened.

Manda: At least tell me you'll be all right.

Manda: And if I need to hunt them down.

> Me: I'll be fine. I promise.

Someone knocked. Was it them?

Fuck me for thinking that.

I forced myself to stay angry as I peeked through the peephole.

My father was on the other side of the fisheye lens, glancing one way down the hall and then the other.

Fuck him too.

I yanked the door open. He was about to hear exactly what I thought of him. Again.

Like that had ever done me any good.

"Brienne. Hi." His voice was kind and even.

"What?"

"I was hoping we could talk. I'm worried about you."

Now? After nearly twenty-eight years? I found that hard to believe. "Uh-huh."

"I'm not here to fight." He was using the tone he typically reserved for dealing with me in public.

"I am." In fact, I was looking for a fight. "So you need to go someplace else if that's not what you want."

"What I want is to help. I know what Dad is leaving you, and it's a huge burden. I want to make sure you have the assistance you need."

For spending his father's money? I was pretty sure I had it. "Go. The fuck. Away."

"Brienne. Sweetie. Be reasonable."

Be reasonable. The number of times I'd heard that growing up. When I wanted to learn piano and he got me math tutoring instead. When I wanted to go to the amusement park with my friends for my birthday, and he made me get my hair and makeup done and go to the country club to hang out with the boys instead.

Be reasonable.

"You were asked to leave." Kenzie's voice came from behind him.

Really?

"Now." That was Scott. He and Kenzie rounded the corner and came into view.

Dad looked between them and me. "I see."

What did that mean? I'd ask, but I refused to give him any satisfaction.

I hated seeing Kenzie and Scott here. Even more because not all of me was upset by it. They joined us, and stepped between Dad and me.

"Is this going to continue to be a problem?" Scott asked.

"Not for me, no." Dad stepped back, and then walked away.

Kenzie handed me the street clothes I'd worn this morning. She had changed out of her dress as well. "Can we come in?" She asked.

I wasn't setting myself up for more hurt. "No."

"Do you want us to leave?"

Yes. I couldn't force the word out in response to Kenzie's question.

"We can do this in the hallway, that's fine." Did Scott even know what *this* was, or had Kenzie given him a sob story about how she was the victim and I was being mean?

Not that I'd ever seen her do that.

The uncomfortable look she wore now though, at the idea of having a conversation like this where others could hear, that was familiar.

Good.

"We would've been here sooner, but I had to get your address," Scott said. "And then we had to find where it actually was."

It was a reasonable excuse, as much a s I didn't want it to be.

"Manda wouldn't tell me where you lived, so we had to call Chloe," Kenzie added.

Good for Manda. "Because she's a friend."

Kenzie frowned.

"As opposed to someone *who works for my husband's VP.*"

Scott clenched his jaw.

"I'm sorry. I'm trying to tell you that. Please talk to us." Kenzie sounded sincere. Almost desperate.

And? "We're talking now." I realized she wanted to take this inside, and I didn't want to do it in front of the neighbors either. But there was a sick satisfaction in making her feel a fraction of what I had at the ren faire, hanging out with her.

"I froze." Kenzie twisted her fingers together in front of her and pulled them apart again. "With Barb. My mind went blank and I didn't know what to tell her. You and I have never had that conversation."

"It would've been great if *friends* was your first idea and not an afterthought."

Kenzie never looked away from me, to her credit. "Is that all we are?"

"We're not even that anymore. You could've just asked. At any point."

"So could you," Scott said.

He was right and I hated him for it.

It was enough of a reasonable statement to make me yield. I stepped aside and opened the door wider.

They moved into my apartment.

"Do you want to sit?" My inner hostess appeared out of a habit I thought I'd squashed years ago.

Scott jammed his hands in his pockets. "Do you want us to stay?"

I didn't know. "I assume you have thoughts on this."

"Believe it or not, I know not everything is about me."

"I misspoke with Barb," Kenzie said. "I want to make that right. I'll call her now and tell her exactly what we are. I made a mistake, but I want to make it right."

Sure. "You'd call her and tell her we're dating."

"Are we?" The lilt of hope in Kenzie's question almost cracked the brick wall I was building around myself.

I shook my head. "No." But we could've been. I still wanted—

"I can't call you my girlfriend if we're not." Kenzie crossed her arms.

"I don't know why I'd been with someone who's embarrassed to tell people how she knows me." Was I the one who wasn't being fair?

"You're not being fair." Scott might as well have read my mind.

And it pissed me off more. "Of course you're taking her side."

"I'm not taking anyone's side. She fucked up, and now you're fucking up in retaliation."

"Or I fucked up previously and I'm fixing my mistake." I could talk this out with them. I was aware of that. But the ache was still there. That shock from how Kenzie defaulted to introducing me, and that meant I'd opened myself to being hurt. That meant it could hurt more in the future.

I didn't want to fall down a hole that meant my heart would break. I was tired of that.

There was no reason to be a total bitch though. I was capable of compromise. "This was a lot of fun, don't misunderstand. But it's not going anywhere. It never really could've gone beyond what it was, and I'm hoping we can walk away from this and still be friendly."

Not friends. Not that close. That would still hurt. But polite enough that we could smile at each other in public.

"Be reasonable," Kenzie said.

Be reasonable. My father's voice overlapped with Kenzie's in my mind. "I'd like you to leave now." I opened the door again.

"Don't—"

I glared at Scott. "You have to know why I'm doing this. You of all people. Leave. Now."

Kenzie looked like she was going to protest, but Scott guided her out of the apartment.

I leaned my back against the door and pushed it shut as I sank to the ground.

I was being childish.

That was what my father would say. Would Kenzie say the same? *Let's talk this out like adults. Don't be a child about this.*

Fuck it all, why did this ache so very much?

TWENTY-ONE
SCOTT

You have to know why I'm doing this.

But I didn't. I had no idea why Bri pushed us out.

Sure, I got being angry. We were willing to talk. *She* was willing to talk. And then to cut things short? To shove us away with an *I hope we can be friends.*

I didn't know if I was more furious with Bri for saying it or me for not understanding. Why wouldn't she let Kenzie make this right?

Kenzie was quiet on the ride home. When we got back to the condo, she said, "Can we just stay in the rest of the day? Watch something?"

"Sure." Not that I ever had a problem with that.

"I'll be fine." Her voice was soft. "I just need a few days."

I knew her well enough to see she wasn't fine. What was a guy supposed to do when his wife's heart was breaking? I was pretty sure most marriage advice didn't cover that.

Just as bad, if I thought about it, my heart was too. I already had someone wonderful, and I was missing what had never been with someone else.

Was that fucked up?

Whether it was or not, I didn't want to leave things like this with Bri. I could stand on her front step until she heard me out. Not that it would change her mind; not her. I wanted to do it anyway. For Kenzie.

For Me.

I couldn't let Bri slip away. My mind warred between *push for it and you can have it* and *if you push her you'll lose her forever*.

I hated problems with no solution.

Sunday we were supposed to have lunch with my mother. Kenzie begged off, but promised she'd be okay home alone. I didn't want to leave her like this.

"I'll be fine. Go see your mom. Give her my love. Please?"

Damn it.

I went because I missed Mom and I wasn't helping anyone hanging out at home.

Mom's house was near downtown. I bought it years ago, insisted, and she refused to let me get her anything too big. She said she'd sacrificed too much already in the name of possessions, and she wanted to enjoy a simpler life now.

I parked in the driveway behind her car, walked up to the porch, and rang the bell.

Inside, a dog started barking.

"Come in, unless you're here to rob me." Mom's voice came over the doorbell speaker.

I grinned and pretended to huff. "*Mom.*"

"What? The electronics are worth the most. Don't touch the stuff on the far wall or I'll find you myself and hunt you down. My kid made those."

I let myself into the house with a key and the correct code. *The far wall* was her scrapbook of articles about me. I could compare it to the way my father tried to get me to follow in his shoes, but Mom focused on the things I'd wanted to work for.

Her corgi waddled up to me with a bark and a yip, and I crouched to scratch behind his ears. "Where's Mom, Indiana?"

He yipped and turned toward the hallway, wandered a few feet, then came back to make sure I was following. Which meant she was probably in her craft room. I let Indiana lead me in that direction, and sure enough, I found her working on a new quilt design.

"I'm sorry. I meant to wrap this up before you got here." Despite the words, she continued to lay out a series of brightly colored, geometric patterns.

"Don't stop on my account. It looks good."

"You're so sweet." She rose and gave me a careful hug, working not to disturb her layout. "Sit. Talk. Help me finish and then I'll make us lunch."

It was nice to be home. It didn't matter that I hadn't grown up in this house, it was a family home now.

"How have you been?" Mom worked with her pieces, making sure she had them marked and in order before picking them up.

"Busy."

"Same as always, then?"

I chuckled. "Pretty much. Kenzie's sorry she couldn't make it. She sends her love."

"Love and kisses back." Mom reached for another block, this one already sewn together.

This was where one of us would fill the silence with some story. Whatever had our thoughts at the moment, but she was distracted and apparently so was I.

She glanced up after a moment, and studied me. "What's up?"

"Nothing's up. I wanted to visit. Here I am. A guy can't visit his mom?"

"You're always welcome, but something's going on."

I think I'm falling for someone who isn't my wife, and it's okay because Kenzie knows, but it's not okay because this other person just brushed us off. No one brushes me off. That wasn't why I was here. "I need to ask your permission for something."

"You don't need to ask my permission for anything, and you never really have. Even when you were supposed to."

That made me smile again. "This thing I do. I have an offer to write a book."

"About programming? Video games? What kind of book? How exciting."

"Like a memoir. About the game. About me."

"Even more exciting. Do you need pictures of the wall? I told you saving those articles would come in handy."

I might need that later, even if it was simply to check the accuracy of stories I'd told so many times, the details had become muddled in my head. "Parts of the story will be about you. I don't want to tell them if you're not okay with it."

The smile she gave me was broad and pride shone in her eyes. "Your father loved to be seen. Still does. I used to worry you were learning that from him, but no. You don't want to be seen for the sake of being seen, you want to be seen for you."

It was true, but I'd never thought of it that way before. "I'm not sure what your point is."

"Tell this story, and that will happen. Of course, some will interpret it wrong, but that's always the case. I'm okay with you doing that because the fact that you're here means you care how people will see me at the end of the day too. Me, Kenzie, Zach, and anyone else in your circle."

"Thanks. I think." As in, I was going to be pondering the odd tangent for a while. "Where did that come from?"

She turned back to her quilt. "Don't know. Just felt like you needed to hear it, and I meant it. Hold this up so I can pin the other half." She handed me a large section of quilted blocks.

I took the piece from her and held it as directed, but my mind was on her words. Another thing Bri and I had in common: *you want people to see you for you.*

I needed to get her to hear Kenzie out. To listen to me.

"Come back." Mom tapped me on the forehead with her index finger.

I stashed the thoughts in the back of my mind, and marked them for *investigate further later*. "I'm sorry, what?"

"I'm done. You can hand it over. Wherever you drifted off to, I hope it was full of wonder."

Not the kind I was looking for, but, "I think it's getting there." I hoped. I had to make this right.

TWENTY-TWO
BRIENNE

THE FIRST HALF OF THE WORK WEEK WOULD BE FILLED with meetings and prep and rehearsals for SXSW. Chloe headed up all of our convention planning, and that meant I'd be with her taking notes and doing everything else she needed.

I wouldn't have time to look at anyone else or talk to anyone else, especially the head of the company.

Thank God for small favors.

We'd fly to Austin on Thursday. This year was a big announcement for us, and it was tech based, so I needed to be there and so did Scott, but he'd be far too busy to look at me.

And I could keep my distance from him.

Monday, he was in multiple meetings I walked into. But so were a lot of people. I didn't have to make eye contact with any of them, as long as I kept my head down and did my job.

If I looked at him, I might pay more attention to the part of me losing my internal struggle. I might start to believe that pushing Kenzie away was stupid. Pushing Scott away was stupid.

I couldn't believe that, because falling for either of them was stupider. There would be no falling here. By the end of Monday, I'd managed to avoid any contact with Scott beyond passing nods. Mostly because I made sure I was never alone in a room with him, and I ignored him calling for me to stop as I left the office at the end of the day.

What now?

Going home alone would suck. More the *alone* part than the home part.

I sent Manda a text and asked what she was up to, and we made plans to meet for dinner at a little cafe near her house. The problem with our location was that it sat across the street from the Ren Faire park. Pulling into the neighborhood gave me flashbacks of Saturday, and grief mixed with fury mixed with a regret I didn't want to acknowledge.

Manda was already here and picked us out a table. I couldn't stomach the thought of food, so I grabbed a boba tea and joined her.

She wrinkled her nose when she saw my drink, but gave me a quick hug.

I handed her back the dress she'd loaned me, neatly folded and wrapped in a paper bag. "I'm sorry again about the damage."

"It's all right." She set the package in the empty chair next to her. "Neptune says she can fix it no worries." The pink that spread across her cheeks at *Neptune* was almost as bright as her hair.

"I'm glad."

This place did most of its business during the days in the summer, because it offered such great views of foliage in its own backyard and across the street. This time of year, Manda and I were the only people in here besides the employees.

It was still bright and cozy though, and for a moment, I could pretend the rest of the world didn't exist.

"Kenzie told me what she did." Manda's words were filled with sympathy, but still shattered the illusion of *it'll be all right.*

I didn't want to talk about it, but I also did. I wanted to be vindicated. Or maybe for Manda to tell me I was making a mist—

Nope. Vindication. That was what I chose. "What did she tell you?"

"That she did a crummy job of introducing you to a friend who wasn't as nice as me. That she fucked up and deserved to be raked over the coals for it."

The first part sounded like Kenzie, the second part… "Those were her words?"

"Basically. Are you all right?"

"I'm fine." The more I said it, the more true it would become. "We parted ways amicably, and I told them both we could still be friends."

"Okay."

That was a less than satisfactory reply. I sipped my drink and eyed Manda.

Her response was to take a huge bite of her muffin and stare back.

"What is that? Okay?" I asked.

"A participle? A gerund? I'm pretty sure it's not a preposition. Sentence construction wasn't my strong suit in high school."

Damn me and the fact that editing and proofreading were just a few of the many things required of my job. "It's a noun, at least in this context. That's not what I meant."

"*I* mean, it's okay. How you responded to her. I don't want to see you break again. Not the way you did last time. If this is what's best for you, *okay*."

"Okay then." I stole a bite of her muffin and chewed. The food didn't taste as good as I wanted. Rather, the muffin was fine, but my brain decided *fine* equaled *what is this? Sawdust?*

"You should know…" Manda hesitated.

I glared at her, but couldn't get rid of my mouth full of dryness.

"I had lunch with Kenzie today," she said.

I swallowed my food, and the big lump went down hard. My throat was dry. The muffin was dry. Coughing ensued. I coughed through swallows of tea, and drained two thirds of my cup before I managed to stop. "Why?"

The look Manda gave me was somewhere between sympathy and pity. "She's helping with the zoning for the faire. We went over the initial details today."

"She'll be really good at that." I was okay. We'd just agreed I was okay, and Kenzie and I would still be friends in the future. The lump in my chest was the result of the coughing fit and nothing more.

"She will be, and I'm excited about what she's done

so far. She's so eager to help, and she's going to make some calls for Neptune and her charity drive too. And she knows some people who can help Toad. She knows everyone, did you realize that?" Manda frowned. "Of course you did."

Time to brace myself to hear about Kenzie from all my friends for the next forever. "I'm really glad it's working out." And I was. This was the help Manda needed, and it would give Kenzie a way to step up.

"She also misses you," Manda said softly. "She pulled me aside after and asked how she could make things up to you."

I could say *let's try again* or *I'll hear you out* or *I know it was an honest mistake*. But I couldn't. No. "There's nothing to make up. We're friends, and there's nothing wrong with that." I was lying. I heard the lie in my own voice. "I can't do that again." Fall for someone who would treat me like the last couple did. I couldn't risk it.

"I told her it was up to you," Manda said. "It doesn't matter how sweet or well-connected or hot in that *virgin heroine* kind of way she is. You're my ride or die, so we ride, and she can suck it up."

I gave Manda a grateful smile. "Thank you."

Nothing was resolved, but at least my friends—my real friend who got me and knew who I was—had my back.

Tuesday, I managed to avoid Scott all day.

By the end of Wednesday, things were looking good

as well. Tomorrow morning I'd fly out to Austin, and everyone would be too busy to ask anything of me but my job. Scott would have no time to track me down.

I was sitting in a room after a meeting, making last-minute notes before heading back to my desk. The door opened, and I looked up.

My heart dropped into my feet when I saw Scott walk in and close the door behind him.

I'd finish my notes later. "Do you have this room? I'll leave you to it." I scrambled to scoop up my laptop and dropped my notepad in the process.

He was already sitting next to me. He reached down to grab my dropped paper. When I reached for it, he grabbed my wrist. His grip wasn't tight, but I couldn't look away from his gaze. I couldn't breathe.

"Hear me out," he said.

I needed to get back to work. All I had to do was say those words and pull away. "About what?"

"About us."

"There's no us. I told you and Kenzie—"

"If you want us as individuals, this is about you and me. You can't punish me for her sins."

"There were no sins." And I wasn't holding anything against her. I was removing myself from a situation where I was going to get hurt. "She reminded me of what we all were, and there's nothing wrong with that."

"Bullshit." Scott's voice turned hard. "You and me? We spark bright and hot."

Fucker. "Arrogant asshole."

"You keep saying that, and I won't argue." He

leaned closer. "Tell me I'm wrong." His voice was so soft I barely heard it.

"You're wrong. There are no sparks." I was lying. Could he tell? "If I let you in, you'll try to convince me to forgive her." I didn't mean to add that

"You already said there was nothing to forgive. And I *will* try to get you to hear Kenzie out, because she's sorry."

I shook my head. "It doesn't matter. I'm not interested in either of you for something long term. We had fun, and it's over now. Friendship should be enough." Shouldn't it? I didn't even believe myself. I wanted him to push so I could hate him for it.

He squeezed tighter. "Friendship isn't enough."

Now I could be angry. "Let go of me, or I'll scream."

"I'll help."

"You'll help me scream?" I faltered.

"Yes. And then I'll tell everyone that you captivate me. That you light my mind on fire and remind me of why I do the things I do and why I choose so often to tell the world to go fuck itself. I'll tell anyone who will listen that you and I could be more. The three of us could be everything. You. Me. Kenzie. And I don't care who hears it, because I want everyone to know."

This was terrifying. His passion was terrifying.

The fact that I wanted everything he just said was terrifying.

Because I couldn't get hurt again. Not like last time. I couldn't go through that pain that nearly ripped me apart last time and that I was willing to surrender myself to.

The three of us.

I pulled out of his grasp and stood. "No. I need to get back to work. I'll see you in Austin, Mr. McAllister."

TWENTY-THREE
SCOTT

WE'D BEEN PLANNING THIS FOR MORE THAN A YEAR. IT was new and exciting and it lit my imagination on fire. In thirty minutes, Chloe would make the announcement on stage, and I'd step up and get into the technical stuff.

She and I were in a room near the Tech Track main hall, with Judith and Elliot, making sure everyone had the last minute details straight.

Our phones were ringing, but we were all too focused on the task at hand to pay attention. Whatever it was, whoever it was, there were other people who could handle emergencies. At least for the next couple of hours.

I should be here in this moment and nothing else, but I couldn't ignore the nervous tension building in my gut. Things weren't right. With Bri. With Kenzie…

Was there more to this bad feeling, or was I letting real life leak into work?

Who was I kidding? When had the two not overlapped?

There was a knock on the door, and Bri stepped into the room. My entire body reacted, heat and need and possessiveness spilling through me. *Not now.*

"We have a problem." She didn't wait for anyone to ask her what was up, but she got everyone's attention instantly with those simple words.

"What's going on?" I asked.

She had her phone in her hand, and unlocked the screen. "My father's company just put out a press release. They've announced a piece of game security software…" She read aloud from the press release.

"Fuck," Elliot muttered.

The language wasn't the same as our presentation, but the meaning was.

"I have an email from him, too," Bri said. "If we have anything similar in the pipelines, because I've been *secretly* working for you, he'll see us in court."

"Are you fucking kidding me?" Judith was mad.

I didn't blame her.

"I'm sorry." Bri's quiet tone and bowed head were very unlike her.

Chloe stepped forward. "No. Don't you dare apologize for him. This isn't your fault."

"Chloe's right." As I spoke, Elliot cleared his throat. I shot him a glare. He'd promised he didn't want details or care what Bri and I had been up to the other night, and this wasn't related anyway. "This isn't the worst case scenario. It's not like the product becomes invalid."

Judith clenched her jaw. "But it is like we can't go out there and announce it. Not today. Months of planning…"

She didn't have to finish the thought—we all knew what she meant.

"Now what?" Elliot asked.

I didn't have an answer. Fuck, fuck, fuck. Another problem without a solution. We'd hyped something big for this conference. Sure, we could go out there and bomb. Say *ha, never mind. We don't have anything.* Failure was always an—

No, it wasn't. Failure was never an option. Not for me. I couldn't knowingly send my people on the stage, or walk out there myself, and say we didn't have anything to announce.

Even if it was true.

This was a bigger problem than today, though. This was the current frustration of my career. We didn't have *anything* new. It was all old. It was all mundane. "We don't have anything else." Saying the words out loud sounded like failure.

"But don't you?" Bri asked.

TWENTY-FOUR
KENZIE

THE ENERGY AROUND ME WAS TANGIBLE. I WAS IN THE first row, waiting for the Rinslet announcement, and I swore the excitement was its own high.

I didn't usually come to these shows, but Scott had been so excited, and this was someplace new to visit. The trip should be a great distraction from Bri, from how much I missed her, but she never left my thoughts.

Would it be a big deal to tell the world we were dating? Or at least to not hide it?

What was the worst people could do? Talk?

When I met Scott, his antics used to horrify me. How could anyone be okay with drawing that much attention to themselves? I'd learned that was who he was and I was okay with it.

But with Bri, it wasn't just about her. I was exposing myself to the world. I had to be okay with that.

Was I?

I should be. It should be as simple as saying I didn't care what people said or thought.

Was I thinking that way because I missed her so much?

No. Bri wasn't just a spark in my life, she saw *me*. She let me be *me*.

My phone chirped with a new text.

> Scott: Change of plans. Not a big deal.
> Just a heads-up.

Why was he sending me this? Sure, I'd spent months watching from the sidelines, but I wasn't part of these decision making processes.

Around me, his name bubbled up in the whispers and murmurs. Rinslet's name was there over and over. It could be because they were all here for the news, but this felt different. Something was off.

At exactly the top of the hour, Scott stepped onto the stage, and a hush fell over the whole room. Why was he up there? Why was he opening this announcement? Sure, he'd been on the schedule to talk, but lead-in was Chloe's job.

As I watched him, along with the rest of the crowd, a flash of movement at the side of the stage caught my attention. *Bri*. My heart did a leapy jumpy dance, before she stepped out of sight again.

"May I have your attention." Scott's voice boomed over the sound system, and all other noise in the room stopped.

It was pretty sexy the way he commanded attention like that.

"I know you're all here for a special announcement, and I'm going to give you exactly that," Scott said.

What was going on? Sure, he worked without a script, but a lead-in like that was vague. The verbal version of click-bait. The lack of substance could mean anything, and that wasn't usually his style.

"I've partnered with a new game company."

Wait. He had? Since when?

"So new, no one's heard of them," Scott continued, and every eye was fixed on him. Every ear pointed in his direction. "So ground-breaking, you haven't seen anything like this since Rinslet came on the scene. So hot, the reality of it will scorch your fingertips."

I'd never seen a more captive audience, and I didn't blame them. I thought I knew what was coming today, and this had me transfixed.

"Stay tuned." Scott walked off the stage.

What the…?

The house lights came on.

The entire room erupted in noise.

Maybe no one else here could get answers, but I could. I stood along with the rest of the crowd, but my destination was the room where Rinslet was set up for ops.

"Hey. I know you. You're his wife." Someone nearby pointed at me, and several other people turned.

Like that, the crowd pressed in on me instead of moving toward the doorway. They shouted questions at me about what was going on. They grabbed for me if I didn't give them attention.

This was literally one of my worst nightmares come to life. "I don't know any more than you. I'm sorry." My reply didn't reach above the din in the room.

"Kenzie." Link was next to me, the crowd he'd parted to get here closing in behind him. "They sent me to find you."

Link was big enough he made Scott look average sized. He was also the sweetest person in the world unless he was pissed off. And I had never been more grateful to see one of Scott's developers.

"What's going on?" I wasn't going to get an answer here, but I had to ask.

He used himself as a wall, as much as one person could, and led me toward the exit. "They'll tell you. I'm just the muscle today."

Okay.

The crowds moved for Link, or they got pushed aside. People shouted questions at both of us. If Scott's goal today had been to start a riot with lack of information, he may have just succeeded.

"Does Scott's weird behavior have anything to do with the fact that you're fucking another woman?" The question hit my back.

What? My footsteps faltered.

"Come on." Link urged me forward again.

A moment later, we were in the room, and the noise was on the other side. Who asked that? How did they know? Or were they just guessing?

Being in here was like stepping into another world. If Scott and his executive team had any idea what was going on, it didn't show. He stood at the front of the room spitting out technical jargon, and they bounced off him. He was animated. More excited than I'd seen him about work in a long time.

Elliot seemed to be agreeing with everything he said, while Chloe and Judith looked more skeptical.

At least that was business as usual.

Bri was here too, sitting at the table, fingers flying over her laptop keyboard as they talked.

I wanted to let them do whatever they were doing, but I had to know. "What was that?"

The look Scott gave me was pure joy. "We were sniped. Chester Jr beat us to the punch with a product that may not even exist."

"Why are we so happy?" Not that I hated this mood. It was contagious and I didn't even know what it was about.

"We're making a new game," Elliot said.

They were what? "Like that?"

"No. Not like that." Judith's tone was cooler. "They're talking about a new company. A spin-off. Only the loosest connections to Rinslet. They're talking about splitting up some of the greatest minds in gaming. Cannibalizing a brilliant organization to build something unknown." The longer she talked, the more her hesitation fell away. By the end of her reply, she was almost smiling.

We were in the Twilight Zone. Rod Serling was saying something off screen that we couldn't hear.

"You're all insane," Chole said.

Elliot grinned. "You love insanity."

Chloe shook her head. "Nope. Don't want any part of this."

"Too late." The lift in Elliot's voice was smug.

"Phillip gave us those renders. *Your* team. You're already a part of it."

Chloe let out an exaggerated groan, but she didn't look upset either.

"Do you love it?" Scott asked me. "It's fucking incredible."

I still felt like I was missing some vital pieces, but their enthusiasm was contagious.

My phone chirped. While I was reaching for it, Bri's did too.

My message was from Barb.

> Barb: Is it true?

My gut sank, though I wasn't sure why. I clicked the link attached to her message, and a website loaded. The entire room fell away, and I was focused on a headline that said I was having an affair with Chester Jr's daughter.

They didn't even use Bri's name. They didn't use mine. *Scott McAllister's Wife...*

And the news was out there. Bright and disgusting and sensationalized, for the world to see.

Bri closed her laptop and stood abruptly. "I need to go."

TWENTY-FIVE
BRIENNE

YOUR GRANDFATHER ISN'T DOING WELL. HE MAY NOT MAKE it through tomorrow.

That was the message from the woman Kenzie put me in touch with at the hospice.

Grandpa was dying. Not just *soon* but *now*.

My mind was a blur as I pushed back from the table. Nothing anyone said mattered. The way Kenzie stared at me didn't matter.

I had to get out of here. I had to get home.

I was halfway through packing up at the hotel when I realized I hadn't told anyone why I was leaving. I had a handful of texts from Chloe, Kenzie, and even Scott. All variations of *Are you all right?*.

I sent Chloe back a reply. *My Grandpa is dying. I have to get home.*

Typing the words, pulling them out of my head, clawed at my throat and my eyelids.

I checked out of the hotel and hopped on the

airport shuttle. There was nothing to do but think, and I didn't want that. I couldn't have that.

Chloe's response came through. *That's fine. Let me know what I can do. Take all the time you need.*

Right. All the time I needed.

I couldn't grasp a single thought long enough to know what it meant. Changing out my return flight was a blur. Going through security. Boarding the plane with the throngs of other people doing the same.

The three hour flight took both an eternity and passed in a blink. As soon as we landed in Salt Lake, I called my contact at the hospice. "I just got into town. I was in Austin. I know your visiting hours are ending for the day..."

"I'll wait for you," she said. "Of course, I'll be here."

I headed straight for the hospice, and left my luggage at the front desk while they showed me to Grandpa's room.

She knocked, but pushed inside without waiting for an answer.

My stomach lurched when I saw Dad standing by Grandpa's bed.

"What's she doing here?" My father growled. "I left explicit instructions—"

"To keep me from seeing my grandfather, I know." I wasn't letting him turn this into drama. For once in his fucking life, couldn't he see this wasn't about him. "You can leave the room while he and I talk."

Dad sneered. "You slutty, little—"

"Enough. Leave the room, Junior." Grandpa's voice

was sharp and clear. Strong like the man I'd grown up with.

Dad opened his mouth.

"Now," Grandpa said.

The woman with me gestured to the door. "You can wait in the lobby until they're done. I can ask our order- lies to keep you company if you'd like to make a scene."

Dad hated making a scene. He hated anyone knowing he didn't have control. It was one of the reasons I was such a disappointment to him.

"I'll let you see him." Dad walked from the room.

The woman closed the door behind him, leaving me with Grandpa.

"Hi, Princess." Grandpa reached out a hand.

I ignored that and wrapped him in a huge hug, careful not to jostle any wires or tubes. Tears squeezed from the corners of my eyes, and the raw ache in my chest grew. I wouldn't cry. Not here. Not now.

Grandpa rubbed my back and returned the hug. "It's okay. You'll be okay."

"This isn't about me." My laugh was curt and bitter. "You won't be okay."

"No, I will. I'm about to be in less pain than I have been in years."

I didn't know if that made me want to laugh or cry. "I guess that's one way to look at it."

"That's the way I want you to look at it," he said. "You've always seen the world through a unique lens, and I'm sorry I didn't do a better job of stopping your father from trying to scrub that out of you. I'm so proud of you for not letting him tear you down."

There were times… I didn't want to dive into those memories. My mind and heart were already overloaded.

"I'm so proud of you," Grandpa said. "Of who you are and what you are. Don't mourn me. Spite me, spite your father, by continuing to live. Tell death to go fuck himself, and keep being you."

This time I did laugh. It was a dark, strangled sound, but it was twisted amusement. "I love you, Princess." Grandpa's voice was getting tired. Weak. He pressed his lips to my forehead.

I stayed there, half-laying, half-hugging him, until he drifted off to sleep and the nurse made me leave.

Numbness sank in on the ride home. I replayed the conversation again and again in my head, overlapped with the memories. When I was back at my place, I pulled out the photo albums and found the directories on the cloud with pictures of me and Grandpa.

There weren't as many as I wanted, but the handful out there soothed the pain growing in my chest.

I wasn't sure when I drifted off, but a phone call at about two in the morning woke me up.

"Your grandfather passed away about two hours ago —" Anything else they said was a mumbled blur. At least to my brain.

I was pretty sure I thanked the person calling before I hung up. And I cried. I cried until everything hurt and I was out of tears, and then I kept going.

A pounding on my door yanked me from a rough sleep. It took me a moment to focus dry eyes on my phone. Seven in the morning.

I couldn't deal with this.

The hammering stopped.

It started again a heartbeat later. "Bri, I swear to god if you're home, you need to talk to me."

That was Manda. She wouldn't care if I had mascara smeared on my face and bloodshot eyes. I dragged myself from the couch, and unlocked the door.

"How are you not freaking out about—" Manda stopped when she saw me.

I turned away. "About what?" I was too drained for this.

"About the gossip. About Kenzie… What's wrong? What happened?" Manda's voice and footsteps followed me back to the couch.

I sank into the cushions again. "My grandpa died last night." I must be all cried out. I managed the words without tears, but saying them still made my throat raw all over again.

"No. I'm so sorry." Manda settled next to me and wrapped her arms around me.

Nope. The tears were back.

"I know I didn't see him much." I stuttered between sobs. "But he was family. He was the only family I had who cared."

"I know. I'm sorry." Manda held me. Rubbed my back.

We stayed like that until I had myself together enough to sit up again. "I don't…" I didn't know what to say.

"It's okay. Go wash your face. Take a shower if you can. I'll make breakfast." Manda pushed me toward the bathroom.

I zombie-walked through cleaning up. A part of my brain registered that she'd said something about Kenzie. About gossip. I needed to grasp onto that, because I couldn't dwell in grief like this.

I'd known this was coming with Grandpa. Maybe not when, but he hadn't been well for a while. I should've been more prepared for it. It still hurt though.

When I emerged from the bathroom, Manda had food on the table. Pancakes and eggs and coffee.

"Thank you." I could say that much. I could manage that level of politeness. But I didn't know if I could eat.

We sat there for a few minutes, with her picking at her food and me staring blankly at mine. "Put forkfuls of sustenance in your mouth, or I'll do it for you," Manda finally said.

Fine. "Yes ma'am." The first bite hit my stomach hard, and the follow-up drink didn't help. Was I going to be sick?

My tummy growled.

No, apparently, I was starving.

"When did you eat last?" Manda asked while I stuffed my face.

"I don't know. What time is it? Yesterday morning. I got the call right before lunch, and there was chaos before that, and all the execs were panicked. And Kenzie—" My brain was waking up, but it stuttered on the thought. "What did you say about her?"

Manda sighed. "It's why I came over. It's all over social media, and apparently there are pictures and eye-witnesses talking about how you had an affair with your boss's wife."

I faltered and my gut lurched. "What is she saying?" This was a bad time for this to happen. I couldn't focus on something so stupid. So insignificant. I needed the distraction though.

"Nothing. She hasn't responded," Manda said.

No. I had a family member to mourn, and couldn't deal with something that had been a fling.

It wasn't a fling. I want her here. I want them here.

"Where's my phone?" I pushed back from the table.

Manda scrambled to her feet. "I think I saw it on the coffee table. What are you—" She sprinted in front of me and snatched the device up before I could grab it. "There is no reason you need that right now."

"I do." I grabbed the phone back from her and opened a social media app. The number of notifications and private messages glared back at me. There were even more on the company page. A click in showed me my name on several of them.

Manda took my phone again. "This is a bad time for you to be reading messages. What are you trying to do?"

Make myself even more miserable. She was right, though. "I want to post a response to the news."

"I'll type it for you. What do you want to say?"

Hooking up with Kenzie was one of the best things I ever did. And Scott. Calling it an affair is a gross misstatement and you all need to grow the fuck up and leave us alone. "I want it to say that the rumors aren't true. I didn't have an affair with a married woman. I don't have feelings for Kenzie." I almost stalled on the words. "There's nothing else to say about the matter, please let me grieve."

Manda stared at me.

"Do you need me to repeat it?" I didn't mean to snap.

She shook her head and tapped at my screen. "I'm going to delete all the messages on your timeline and in your inbox that aren't nice. You can't stop me."

I didn't have the energy to do so.

Manda basically moved in for the next few days, and I was grateful for it. Flowers arrived from work. From a few friends. Manda passed along more sympathies from our circle of friends.

When a basket of chocolate croissants from a bakery in Park City showed up, I almost lost it. The note said *I know you liked these. You know where to find me if you need me.*

Fuck.

I spent the rest of the time simmering in my own thoughts and preparing for the funeral. It was as much a mental preparation to see my father, and my grandfather's associates, as it was prepping myself for the emotional impact of saying *goodbye.*

I wasn't quite as numb each morning, though sleep was the biggest thing that kept the days from blurring together.

It was the day of the service before I knew it. Walking into the funeral home took a force of will I wasn't sure I had. So many people approached me. Friends of Grandpas who I didn't know. They all wanted to tell me how proud he was of me.

Manda was by my side, and when Scott and Kenzie walked in, she squeezed my hand.

I held on to her with all the strength I had left. Seeing them ached. Not just missing the physical, but as

Scott and Kenzie exchanged polite conversation with everyone, it hit me that I wanted to be facing this with them.

They'd been becoming family. Part of me had already started thinking of them that way.

"Brienne Walker?" The man who approached me was broad shouldered, attractive, and probably about Scott's age.

I had no idea who he was. Presumably an associate or friend of Grandpa's given where we were. "That's me."

"I'm sorry for your loss. He thought the world of you, and coming from him that's high praise."

I wanted to sink into the comfort of the words, and hated that this was a place I didn't dare let my defenses down that way. "Thank you. How did you know him?"

"I'm Dominic. I was his attorney, and I'm the executor of his estate."

Oh. "Pleasure to meet you." It was easier to slide into basics than think of anything more complicated to say.

"Same." He shook my offered hand with a firm grip. "I am sorry to approach you here, about business, but you haven't returned my calls. I will need to speak to you when you're ready."

Right. Because Grandpa left most of it to me. "I can't tell you when that will be."

"That's fine." Dominic handed me his card. "Take your time. I just wanted to make sure you had my number."

"Thank you." I slipped the card into my purse.

I talked to a few more people, all of them kind and offering their condolences. I could do this. It wouldn't be too bad.

"Brienne." My father's cool voice stripped away the heavy blankets I'd piled around my heart over the last week.

"I can't," I said softly to Manda. "I need to go." I tugged her hand.

Scott stepped between Dad and me. "We're sorry for your loss, Chester." Scott's voice was cooler than I'd ever heard it.

"You're sitting with us." Kenzie was next to Manda and me, steering the two of us toward the front row.

I hated that even at a fucking funeral, this had to be about a power play. But I didn't care about the people whispering as Scott sat on one side of me and Kenzie sat next to Manda, the three of them boxing me in.

Let people talk. This was a day to mourn the loss of a great man and fuck anyone who used it for something else.

A few days later, I had to go back to work. Chloe had assured me they'd be fine for as long as I needed, but what I needed was to go back to life. To not sink inside myself. The grief wasn't getting smaller, but it was becoming easier for me to work around.

And losing myself in tasks would help.

The first day back was both rough and a relief. I knew this routine. The whispers and stares weren't great though. I was wrapping up a meeting with Chloe and about to go back to my desk when she said, "If you want me to keep you out of meetings with Scott…"

Tempting. "No. I want things to go back to what they were."

"I'd like to tell you *okay*, but you need to know nothing will be the same."

That was less than encouraging. It was also the most honest and direct thing I'd heard in days. "I know, but there has to be a balance between there and where I am now."

"There is, but it's not what you think it is, and it will hurt to get there," Chloe said. "Anything I can do…"

I shook my head. "I'll ride it out."

The next day when I walked into the cafeteria, it was the same as every other room I'd entered since I came back to the office. The conversation stopped. Everyone stared at me.

I was so sick of this. I climbed onto the nearest table. "*Hey*." No one was going to look away from me now. "Pay attention, because I'm not going to do this again."

A room full of people, including the cafeteria staff, stared at me.

"The rumors aren't what you think. There wasn't an affair. No one cheated on anyone. If you want the truth, just fucking ask me. Otherwise, find something else to talk about."

There was silence, and then the room erupted in chatter again. A few people called my name, but I stalked out of the room.

This sucked. All of it. Missing Grandpa. Missing Kenzie and Scott. I didn't even care what people were saying, I just wanted a life that didn't hurt.

The drive back to my apartment after work was

heavy traffic and tedium. Thank God. It was the best brain drain I'd had in days. I'd sent Manda home the first morning I went back to work, so she could live her life too, and tonight would be turning on the most uninteresting thing I could find, eating ice cream, and not thinking.

I was almost looking forward to my plans as I approached my apartment.

Kenzie was sitting on the ground in front of my door.

My heart ground to a stop. "Why are you here?"

"I thought you might need a friend, and you did say we're still friends."

Go away. Let me be miserable in peace. I don't want this.

I stepped around her, unlocked the door, and offered her my hand. "Come on in."

When her palm met mine, familiarity washed over me and some of my barriers wilted.

TWENTY-SIX

KENZIE

I TRIED TO STAY AWAY BY TELLING MYSELF IT WAS BEST TO give Bri distance. I reminded myself over and over that I'd read into things too deeply and fallen too hard because this was the first real, good thing I'd had since Scott.

I couldn't convince myself of any of that. Letting Bri slip from my life would be a bad idea, and if she was offering friendship, I'd take it. I wanted more. I knew it. With what Bri was going through right now, she needed friends more than some obsessive person hounding her with *love me.*

The rumors would continue, and I'd struggled with that, but not for long. The biggest reason I hadn't made a public statement yet was that I didn't want to deny anything, but I didn't dare do otherwise without talking to Bri first. I'd seen her messages online that there wasn't an affair. That was true in the strictest definition—I'd never lied to Scott about what was going on.

It was Bri's comment of *I have no feelings for…* that tore me up.

Still, I wasn't here for any of that. I was here to see if she needed a friend, and when she invited me in, my heart did little somersaults.

We stepped into her apartment, and she nodded at my hands. "What's in the bag?"

"Presents." I handed her the large sack.

"You don't have to bring me things, to come visit." She left her things by the door, and took the offering from me.

"Don't get used to it," I teased. "But I figured if I were in your shoes, these things would help me."

She moved further into the living room, and after a moment of hesitation, I followed. Her place reminded me of her. Colorful. Decorated to show off who she was. Bright and welcoming.

She set the bag on the coffee table and looked inside, creases marring her forehead. She pulled out a box of cookies.

"They're not homemade." I don't know why I felt like I should explain the obvious, given the box had the store's name on it. I needed to be saying *something*. "But they are warm."

Bri twisted her mouth—in frustration or to hide amusement, I couldn't tell which. Next out was a DVD of old monster movies. *Nosferatu*, *Phantom of the Opera*, and *Swamp Thing*. An odd combination but, "It was that or giant bugs invading Earth, and those tend to require a mood."

That time it was clear, Bri almost smiled. "Yeah, they do."

Last out was an oversized fleece sweatshirt. Bri traced her thumb over the still-folded fabric, and her brow furrowed again. She hugged it and inhaled deeply. "It smells like you."

Heat flooded my cheeks. "It smells like my fabric softener. The tops are comfier if they're washed first, so I did that."

"You don't have one for you."

I ducked my head. "At home. I wasn't sure you'd want me to stay."

"I do."

Such a simple pair of words, but my heart was doing those flippy-happy things again.

"Do you want to sit? I'll be right back." Bri turned toward the kitchen.

"Where are you going?"

"Can't have cookies without milk."

Inarguable logic. "Go put the sweatshirt on. I promise it's like a big warm hug. I'll grab the milk."

"I don't want you getting lost in my kitchen." The glint on her eyes gave away her teasing.

"Believe it or not, It hasn't been very long since I lived in an almost identical floor plan. I can figure it out."

I found the glasses exactly where they should be in the cabinets, and when I returned to the living room a moment later, Bri was emerging from her bedroom.

She looked tiny and fragile in a top that hung to her knees, with sleeves long enough to cover her hands.

Since the first day I'd seen her, she stood strong. Defiant. Tonight, I wanted to protect her and make sure she could heal.

I put the drinks on the table and tugged Bri onto the couch. "Which one do you want to start with?" I asked.

"Whichever one comes out of the box first."

It was a single disc with all three films, so we loaded up *Nosferatu*. It was an hour and a half of cheesy, black and white melodrama. We spent as much time providing our own commentary as we did watching.

As *Phantom* started to play, we were sitting as close to each other as was possible without touching.

"Are you going to ask about it?" Bri's question came from nowhere.

I had a good idea what she meant, but I didn't dare assume and be wrong. "Ask about what?"

"You. Me. How to address the rumors. Any of it. All of it."

"I'm dying to." There was no reason to hide that. "But tonight I'm here as your friend, and to be what you need. Everything else can wait."

"If you weren't waiting for my answer, what would you tell the public?" Bri watched me, instead of the on-screen stage.

"I don't have a straightforward answer for that."

"Why not?"

I could try to figure out what she wanted to hear, but I'd spent so much of my life doing that, and with Bri, I didn't have to. The truth might be complicated, and it might rub her wrong, but I had to say it. "If this was about one of the other women I dated—since you said not you dependent—I'd deny the rumors. I'd hide from them and probably laugh them off nervously with Barb and the other wives. I'd pretend everywhere but in the most private places that it never happened."

"Oh." Bri's shoulders fell.

"Since it is you, since I can't actually look at what I feel and not think about you, fuck what they think."

"But really."

I laughed nervously. Fair counter. "Okay, I can't completely convince myself of that. Part of me clenches at the thought of telling anyone to fuck off. But at the same time, I want to. I'm tired of being someone I'm not. I love being with you because you don't do that and you don't expect me to do that. I'm tired of being someone I'm not. I love being with you because of who you are. I love *you* because of who you are and that you let me be me. I want more of that."

"Did you just say...?"

As she trailed off, my own words repeated in my head. Yeah, I'd just said that. Wow. Those words hit hard, and I liked it. "I love you, yes." Saying it again, intentionally this time, felt good. I hadn't even put the feeling into words in my own head, but now that it was out there... "You want the truth? That's exactly how I feel. I miss you. I want you back in my life. I love you." It got easier to say each time, but still felt just as incredible as the first time.

Bri was silent.

Did I screw this up? "I'll tell anyone. I'll tell everyone. Even if you don't say it back, I still feel it. I still mean it. I'm so tired—literally exhausted—from hiding."

Bri licked her lips. "I don't want to love you."

A fist clenched around my heart, but I didn't think she was done talking.

"I never wanted to love you. I wish…"

"What?" I prodded.

"I was going to say I wish Grandpa never asked me to go to that party in his place, but I don't wish that. I don't want to love you, but I do anyway. I fell in love with you and I can't even hate it the way I want to."

"That's good?" It sounded good. Or I was grasping at straws.

"It's good." Bri nodded. "I love you too."

"And now we kiss? That's what they do in the books and movies." I was fumbling my way through everything. It was awkward and uncomfortable and wonderful.

Bri pressed her lips to my cheek. The kiss was soft and sweet and most certainly chaste, and it meant more to me than almost any other kiss. She leaned her head on my shoulder. "Thank you for coming here tonight."

I rested my head on hers, and we fell back into the movie. With her this close, with the comfortable silence, this was as cozy and wonderful as anything ever.

The movie was rolling toward a finale when someone knocked.

"Were you expecting company?" Had I intruded?

Bri was careful extracting herself from me. "Might be Manda. She's been forcing niceness on me." She didn't sound upset.

She crossed the room and when she opened the door, I couldn't see who was on the other side from my angle on the couch.

"Is my wife here?"

Scott.

"She is," Bri said. "Is that a problem?"

"Nope. Just wanted to make sure she made it safely."

I held my breath at Scott's reply. *Please don't let this play out poorly.*

"Are you coming in?" Bri asked.

"Did you save me a cookie?"

Like that, the two of them were talking again. How did they do it?

"No." Bri opened the door wider. "Unless that's a euphemism. But still, no."

Scott stepped inside and flashed me a smile. "How about a seat?"

"Always." Bri led him back to the couch, and I pulled her down between us. She leaned into me, but her feet easily found their way onto Scott's lap.

The jealousy wasn't there. I was glad the two of them could do this. Be so comfortable with each other. That wasn't me, but what I had with each of them was just as good. How did I get so lucky?

Whatever came next wouldn't be easy. It wasn't like tonight would solve everything, but we were on the right path.

And it would all be worth it to keep Bri in my life.

TWENTY-SEVEN
SCOTT

I was going to stay away tonight. I was trying to give Bri time, but I wasn't a patient person, and I wanted—needed—to see her in a setting where meetings and corporate culture weren't an excuse. I would've come over after work even if Kenzie hadn't told me she'd be here.

Swamp Thing was terrible, and I didn't remember ever enjoying a movie more. Bri asked us not to go home at the end of the night. It was crowded in her bed, but it was worth staying, to be next to her.

I was up before either of them the next morning, mostly because I was the only one who had to go home to change before I went to the office. I should leave them with coffee, so I made my way into the kitchen.

The beans and filters were definitely in the wrong place. I was putting the pot on to brew when Bri walked into the kitchen.

She was just as gorgeous rubbing sleep from her eyes as she was commanding control of a conference room at work. She still wore the oversized hoodie from Kenzie, who owned an almost identical one and I was pretty sure lived in it when I wasn't home.

"I thought I got out of bed, but pretty sure I'm still dreaming," Bri said playfully.

It was good to see her smile again. "Why is that?" I asked.

"Sexy guy making coffee in my kitchen?" She pinched me. "Nope, you're real."

I gestured at myself with a smirk. "I'm *all* real, baby. Your fantasies come to life."

She snorted. "Not quite, but it's cute that you think that." She squeezed into the tight space next to me, and grabbed mugs from the cupboard.

Having her so close, playing this way, I let temptation take over. I pinned her between me and the counter. "Nothing to hide behind in here."

"Nothing to hide from." She met my gaze without hesitation.

She felt so good here, under me. I wanted to push. I wanted *her*. She was so close and tempting.

Instead, I stepped away and let her go. In the background, the coffee maker sputtered and hissed water through grounds.

"How are you holding up?" I asked.

She gave me a rueful smile. "It's harder some days than others, but I'm doing all right."

"I'm glad. Not about the hard part." I winced at the unintentional innuendo. "I mean…"

She laughed. "I know what you mean. Thank you."

"You know, we could call in today. Spend the day watching more movies. Fucking around…"

"You have meetings all day."

It was true. Stupid responsibility. "You can't prove that."

"I literally can." She had access to all her calendars, so it was true. "Besides, what would people say if we both called in on the same day?"

Same things they were already saying. People did love to talk. "I heard about what you did in the cafeteria yesterday. I didn't think you cared what people said."

"I do if I lose my job over it."

Not a conversation I'd intended to have now, but it was as good a time as any. Besides, hopefully she'd see this as good news, and she needed some of that. "You're on the board of directors. You *literally* could ask for any job you want." I used her language on purpose.

"That doesn't mean you'd give me said job."

True. Zach and I maintained a lot of control of what we did and who we hired. It wasn't my call in this case, though. "That doesn't mean the hiring manager would give it to you. This is between you and Chloe. Fortunately for all of us, you're incredible at what you do, and it doesn't have to come up."

"Hang on. I have to process that."

Huh? "Process what?"

"What you just said."

I still didn't understand. "Was it confusing?"

"A little. Because I can be with you, I can date you, I can fuck you, I can dump you, and even though you run the company I work for, you can't touch my job."

223

Sounded like she got it just fine.

"I'd rather you not do that last one," I said.

Her playfulness was back. "Don't give me a reason to."

I wrapped an arm around her waist, dipped my head, and dragged my nose up her neck, to nudge her ear. "I don't think you know what you're asking for." I didn't either, but *fuck* if finding out wasn't going to be incredible.

"Surprise me."

"You'd better believe I will." I let her go, amused by her raised eyebrows. I brushed my lips over the back of her knuckles instead. "I need to get home. Get ready for work. I'll see you at the office."

"You're not going to back me into a corner and make me kiss you?"

It was tempting. "Not while you're dealing with this, and never if you don't want it. But it's not off the table in the future."

Her almost-smile was worth so much.

I stopped by the bedroom to give Kenzie a kiss as she woke up. "I'll see you tonight." Hopefully both of them, but I was willing to show the tiniest bit of patience while Bri dealt with grief.

PLANNING a new game was a kind of high I never got enough of, and this one, the idea we floated at SXSW, was newer than anything had been in a long time. We'd spent that entire week in Austin in opening conversations about what we could do. What we wanted to do.

Elliot bought in right away, with the same enthusiasm I had. Not surprising, since he seemed to be working on a lot of this behind the scenes.

He'd already looped in other senior members of our various teams, and I was fine with keeping them onboard as we started the conversation of how to make this happen. I trusted all of them.

After talking to Zach, Kenzie, Elliot, and Judith, we confirmed that the new idea couldn't be a part of Rinslet. The concept deserved more flexibility than our giant could offer, and I deserved someone besides me at the helm, as well.

That was fine. I didn't want to head up a new company; I just wanted to be part of what they were creating.

Elliot was willing to head development and let me *consult* on the side. Judith was considering stepping into the up-top role. She belonged there, and the only thing keeping her from reaching the top at Rinslet was the fact that Zach and I weren't going anywhere.

She was hesitating. Saying she needed to consider every angle. I knew her and that she wanted this. She'd accept, it was just a matter of getting her to see what we saw.

The dual conversation meant my days were more packed than usual with meetings, and I didn't mind one bit. Those meetings with Bri in them were even better. She was quiet at first, but as days passed, she started to speak up more, the way she used to.

She and Kenzie decided not to make a big huge announcement about who they were, but they also weren't going to hide it. When the three of us were out to dinner—and I assumed when it was just the two of them—they'd hold hands. The touches and looks were sweet and intimate.

The next couple of weeks flew by in a hectic whirl-wind, which was status quo. I worked late hours. Kenzie spent more and more time with Bri's friends, helping with smaller causes and those things that didn't usually call for big attention.

I loved seeing Kenzie happier.

And when Bri spent the night, the two of them stayed in the guest room.

I was happy for them. I still wanted Bri though. There had been few things in my life I was willing to bide my time for, but she was at the top of the list.

Nearly a month passed, and impatience won out over being practical. As everyone was leaving one Friday afternoon, I asked if I could see her in my office.

As she stepped into the room, there was an unusual for her hesitation in the way she swung the door back and forth.

"Up to you if you close it or not," I said.

She did, and twisted the lock in place.

Such a simple action, but it was enough to make me half hard. I wasn't sure that was what this conversation was about, but her actions put more intimate options on the table.

"*Now* I want to have this conversation," I said.

"Which one?"

I suspected she knew which one. "The one where we talk about if there's more to you and me. Even I know there are lines, and I haven't wanted to push you."

"Good boy. Do you want a cookie?" Her sarcasm was laced with playfulness.

That was a good sign. "I want *you*."

She bit her bottom lip, and looked up at me through her lashes.

I crossed the room in a few short strides, and placed my hands to the door on either side of her head. My satisfaction sparked at the way her breath hitched and the wide-eyed look she gave me.

"I dream about you." My words came out rougher than I intended. "How you tasted. How you sound when you come. The way you talk back and make me work for every fucking thing."

She searched my face, and I swore eons of possibility flowed between us.

"Are you gonna spank me for being difficult, Daddy?"

Fuck. I thought maybe we'd ease into a conversation of *what next*. Not that I wanted to take things slowly, and not that I was complaining about the fun. "Only if you ask right."

Bri slid her palms up my chest to fist my shirt, leaned in, and bit my bottom lip hard enough to sting. She pulled back before releasing me. "Please?" Her question was lightly sarcastic.

This was where we were going, wasn't it?

Good.

I spun her away from me, to press her front to the door, and pushed up her loose skirt.

She wiggled her ass against me.

It was tempting to yank down her panties and smack both cheeks until they were sparking red. It was also tempting to leave her hanging.

Given I wasn't hanging at all, and every time she ground against my erection, I felt the hum through my entire body, the second option wasn't happening today.

Especially when she glanced over her shoulder, challenge written on her face. "Well?"

Well indeed. I pressed into her back and glided my hand along the curve of her ass, while I kissed up her neck. "Spanking would make too much noise," I murmured. "Speaking of... Whatever you do, don't scream."

"About what?" she taunted.

I slipped my fingers between her legs and teased along the thin strip of fabric covering her.

Her tiny gasp was electrifying.

"Shh, shh, shh." I could be just as cruel as she could. "Some things are harder to justify than others, and fucking in the office is one of them."

Her whimper was worth everything. I danced my touch lightly over the heated patch, occasionally pressing harder. Working over her pussy without ever touching it, until her panties were damp and she was panting.

When I finally slid underwear aside, she was slick and ready for me. It was easy to slip my fingers inside her, and her swallowed grunt mingled with my desire and self-satisfaction.

I pumped in and out of her, harder and faster, until she was clenching and coaxing me. I withdrew and slipped up to her clit, and she bucked against my touch.

Part of me would love to draw this out all night, but the setting and my impatience cut that notion short. I circled her swollen button, and when I found a spot that made her shudder, I focused on it. Each movement she made, each muffled sound, was fuel on a fire.

She ground against my hand, harder, faster, her body doing as much of the work as I was, and she moved one hand to her mouth, biting into her fist, as her entire body shuddered in pleasure.

The frantic fingering slowed as she did, and she pulled away from my touch, turning to face me.

Good. I wanted her to watch while I sucked her juices from my fingers. One at a time. Relishing every lick, before I gripped the back of her head and kissed her hard. Hungrily.

She pushed into the lip lock, crushing her mouth to mine. Giving as good as she got. She dragged her mouth along my jaw. "You're an asshole." Her voice was barely a whisper.

"So you keep saying." Something told me she didn't mean it the way most people would.

Bri cupped my erection through my jeans and half-stroked, half-squeezed.

Jesus fuck. I jerked against her touch.

She pulled her skirt up again, hooked her fingers in the elastic of her panties, and slid the clothing down her legs to step out of them.

"What are you—"

She pressed a finger to my lips. "Shh, shh, shh." How she managed to do that in a mimicking voice, I had no idea. "Whatever you do, don't scream."

Not if it stopped whatever came next from happening. I couldn't take my eyes off Bri as she slid my zipper down. When she gripped my warm cock with cool fingers, I had to bite the inside of my cheek to keep from groaning.

She wrapped her panties around my shaft, and I was greeted to a combination of slick, smooth, and rough. As she stroked me, she watched me the entire time, licking her lips.

Not what I'd expected, but absolutely incredible. I had no choice but to lose myself in her touch. To fall into everything about this moment, until I was fucking her hand and fisted panties. The harder my hips worked, the tighter her grip grew.

She gripped me and teased me and coaxed me as need tightened in my balls. And she continued to hold my gaze as climax rose inside, then spilled out. I rested fisted hands against the door, to steady myself, and shuddered, humping her hand until I was spent.

When she loosened her grip, the fresh sensation sent a shiver over me. She was tender wiping me clean, but each new touch on my now hyper-sensitive skin was delicious torture. When she was done, she balled up the panties.

"Damn, now they're ruined." Bri sounded anything but disappointed, as she shoved the wadded up cotton into my pocket.

"I disagree. There is nothing wrong with this scenario."

Her pout was exaggerated. "Except that now I have to drive home all by myself without panties on. Me and my bare, slick—"

"Be at the condo in thirty minutes." I nipped at her neck. "Or else."

"Or else what?"

Was everything a challenge with her? Probably one of the many things I loved about her. "Nothing. Or else nothing." I assumed the threat-slash-promise of me not doing anything to her would be enticing.

She smirked and reached behind her for the doorknob.

I grabbed her wrist.

"Do you want to put that away before I open the door?" She nodded at my cock.

"Yeah. Probably in a minute. But that's not the important thing." Now that the urgency to feel her, to connect with her on a more primal level, was sated, I did have something else I needed to say. "I actually didn't call you up here to trade orgasms."

"No?"

"No." I cupped her face more gently this time. "After I met Kenzie, I never thought I'd say this again. Not in this way. Though with you it's not quite the same, but it is just as intense."

Bri covered my hand with hers. "It must be pretty important to make you dance around the point."

"It is. *You* are. So important. This beacon in my life that makes me remember who I am and what matters.

You're smart and fun and *fucking sexy*, and—" This shouldn't be so difficult. All I had to do was say it. "I love you, Brienne Walker. In a way I've never loved anyone else. I love you even when we're just hanging out and being friendly. I love everything about you."

She leaned into my touch and stroked her thumb over my fingers. "Me too. I mean, I love you back. I mean… Yeah, that's what I mean. I love you too. I just don't have pretty words for it."

"You don't have to." I brushed my lips over hers. "It means the world to me to hear you say it at all."

TWENTY-EIGHT

BRIENNE

THE LAST FEW WEEKS WITH KENZIE HAD BEEN incredible. And Scott, it was easy to poke him, but I was grateful he hadn't pushed me before today. I doubted I would have reacted well, and I did love both of them, in their own ways.

Two distinct individuals, who I got to fit together with like a perfect little puzzle.

I had also spent a decent amount of time talking with Dominic about Grandpa's estate. He'd assured me there were ways to make sure I was comfortable without having to be responsible for all that money, and to ensure it went to things I wanted it to go to, and my father couldn't touch it.

I pulled into the parking garage of the condo. Kenzie's car was in its spot, but Scott's wasn't.

I'd spent enough time here over the last month that I had the code to the building, and most of the security and other staff knew me. I headed upstairs without an issue, and rang the bell.

Kenzie answered, her expression a mix of surprise and happiness. "What are you doing here? Not that I mind. Don't leave or anything." She grabbed my wrist.

I gave her a quick kiss. Those came easily, naturally, now, but they hadn't stopped feeling wonderful and new and incredible. "I was ordered here."

"By...? Never mind. Does that mean you wouldn't be here otherwise?"

"I can't stay away. If you didn't already realize that, allow me to introduce you to the idea that I'm addicted."

The elevator door chimed behind me, and Kenzie's gaze drifted. I didn't need to look to know who it was, since they had the one penthouse suite on this floor. Besides, turning would probably give Scott some sort of satisfaction, and where was the fun in that?

He pressed into my back, startling me. "Why are we in the hallway?" he asked.

Kenzie raised her brows as she looked at us. "Waiting for you, apparently."

Scott nudged us both inside, and closed us off from the rest of the world.

"So this is..." Kenzie continued to study us.

I felt better every day. There were still moments—hours, days—when the grief hit and I missed Grandpa so much. But overall I felt more like myself, and Kenzie was a huge part of that.

I couldn't hide my grin now. This was a new kind of giddy. I grabbed Scott's hand. "Kenzie, this is my new boyfriend. Scott, this is my girlfriend." I was a dorky fucking goof, and it felt incredible.

Scott let go of me to take Kenzie's hand. "Pleasure to meet you." It looked like he was going to kiss her fingers, and instead wrapped his other arm around her waist and dipped her.

She squealed, and he silenced her with a kiss. When he lifted her back to her feet, she looked at me. "I like him. Good choice."

"I like him too. Pretty sure it's love. I think I'm going to keep him." Saying that felt so good, and it was even better that I could say it to her without hesitation.

"That's smart," Kenzie said. "That's what I'd do. Wait, that's what I did."

"Ladies, ladies. There's enough of me to go around." Scott led both of us farther into the home.

I let out an exaggerated huff. "Just like a guy. Always thinks it's about his dick."

Scott scoffed. "I've seen the two of you tongue wrestle. I *know* it's not all about my dick. It's a good thing I don't have an ego, or that might hurt my feelings."

Kenzie laughed as loudly as I did.

"What?" Scott's confusion looked anything but sincere.

"I can't even imagine you without an ego." Kenzie shook her head.

He grinned. "Lucky for you, I have a good imagination."

"Okay, serious for like two point five seconds, and then you can go back to being you." Despite Kenzie's words, she looked like she was trying to keep a straight face.

I tried to adopt a similar look. "Listening."

"I assume this means the two of you are…" Kenzie trailed off.

Scott nodded. "We said the words. We did the deed."

"Yes, we're officially together," I said.

Kenzie's grin was wonderful. "It's about fucking time."

This was incredible, and exactly where I wanted to be. Kenzie and Scott were family. They cared about me. It wasn't just about the sex, and I trusted them. I could lose myself in them.

And they'd still be there on the other side, every time. I had no doubt of that.

There was no more wonderful feeling.

WAKING up next to Kenzie and Scott, in their bed, was a kind of incredible I could get addicted to. We hadn't all been together like this since that first night I kissed Scott. Since Kenzie almost pushed me away because of jealousy, and I nearly cut them out because I refused to be used as a marital aid.

Thank God we worked through that.

They were both rousing as well, and as much as I wanted to lay here all day and relish the cuddles, my stomach was grumbling. "What's for breakfast?" I asked.

"Me," Scott said.

Should I be surprised by an answer like that? Probably not.

"Wherever we're going, do we have time for me to take a shower?" Kenzie asked.

Scott sat up, letting the sheets fall away from him. "We could all take a shower. It's big enough."

I let out an exaggerated huff. "Are you always this insatiable?" Some days it might be an issue, but this morning, I wanted to enjoy them both.

"No. Put a complex problem in front of him, and he'll completely stop thinking about sex," Kenzie said.

I doubted Scott was any less irresistible when that happened. I loved seeing him solving problems.

I scrunched my face up. "So my choices are—give him a problem to solve, and we both probably starve, or shower sex and breakfast?"

"Exactly," Scott said. "There is absolutely no other option at all. In any way."

Far be it from me to point out there were half a dozen other options, and those were just the ones that immediately came to mind. "In that case, lead the way."

None of us wore anything, and watching Kenzie climb from the bed was adorable. She held onto the sheets until the last moment, though we'd both seen her naked plenty of times. The way the pre-dawn light caught her form through the window was stunning. Curves and grace.

Scot had zero shame when he got up, and he was just as much eye candy. No nerd had the right to look that good, especially creeping up on forty.

The three of us moved into the master bath. It was odd stepping in here. Like stripping away another layer of intimacy. It didn't matter how many times I'd been here, I'd never dared use this room. Probably a weird superstition, but it was what it was.

Scott had understated how big the shower was. Room for four or five people to stand around and talk. Perhaps do yoga... Maybe not.

There was a seat in one corner, and all sorts of jets coming out of the walls, plus a removable shower nozzle. *Fun.*

As Scott moved past me, he paused to brush his lips over mine. His body was hot and hard, and I didn't have a choice but to mold myself to every unyielding muscle. Reluctance whimpered inside as he moved away, but watching him steal a kiss from Kenzie was pretty good too.

He turned on the shower, and I slipped into his place to crush my mouth to Kenzie's. As my mouth moved with hers, she backed into the shower, pulling me with her. Water cascaded around us, rapidly heating and spilling over us to mingle with our need.

I lost track of how long we stayed in a lip lock, only breaking apart when Scott snaked in to steal a kiss from one or the other of us. The rest of the time, he alternated between playing with her breasts and sucking on my nipples.

Three way shower make-out session was skyrocketing to the top of my list of favorite things. It felt like time to move on, though. I reached past them to grab the showerhead. "I changed my mind," I murmured against Kenzie's skin, loud enough for both of them to hear.

"About what?" Kenzie bit her bottom lip.

I moved the nozzle between her legs, and she gasped

and widened her stance. Water teased along her core, leaving her squirming and breathing heavily.

"About waiting for breakfast. I want to eat now." I put the showerhead away, and nudged Kenzie until her back met Scott's front. Kissing a row of kisses down her stomach, I relished each new gasp and giggle that escaped her throat.

He moved his hands to her breasts again, and rolled her nipples between his fingers, while I brushed my mouth along her thighs.

When I licked along her slit, Kenzie bucked, but Scott had her mostly restrained.

I licked and explored and enjoyed the way her juices flowed. When I slid two fingers inside her, she bucked at the penetration. I pumped over and over, until her hips swayed in time with my motion, then I wrapped my mouth around her clit to suck.

No one had ever focused so intently on spelling the alphabet with their tongue as I did. Kenzie's cries of pleasure when she came were delicious and my desire soared. I kept sucking and licking while she pressed into my mouth and clenched around my fingers and pulled my hair keeping my head in place.

We finally broke apart and I kissed up her body to share her taste with her in a long, tongue-tangling kiss.

Scott gripped my dreads and yanked me to him, to crush his lips against mine. "Watching is only fun sometimes." His voice was a gravelly growl. "I need to fuck you."

There was no way I could turn that down. I grabbed the condom he'd rested on a higher shelf, ripped it free from its foil, and rolled it onto his cock. The way his eyes rolled back at the teasing contact was its own fresh delight.

Scott spun me away from him, pressed a hand to my back, and bent me slightly. He teased his fingers along my slit, the way he had in his office, but I was far wetter today. Already so far into desire that I would take anything that happened next.

When he thrust his cock inside me, he stretched me out. He buried himself deep, then withdrew to the tip before plunging inside again. The repeated motion, again and again, had me panting with need.

And then he stayed, buried deep, and gripped my hips. I half-closed my eyes as he rocked in me. When I felt a mouth on my pussy, my eyes flew open in surprise.

Kenzie was on her knees in front of me, licking from Scott's shaft up to my clit over and over.

Fuck.

I was caught in an incredible trap, rocking between them. Falling into mounting pleasure. A pressure that crept inside me at first and then surged forward on climax. When I came, it was potent and all-consuming. I was lost in the throes of orgasm when I heard Scott's strangled grunts. Felt his punctuated thrusts.

And when he came, it drew out my own orgasm.

The frantic need slowed as we all collapsed against each other to catch our breath. The afterglow lingered as we cleaned each other off. The entire rest of the shower was a lazy affair filled with as much teasing as cleaning. It was all soapy bodies and slick fingers in sensitive places.

We probably took twice as long as we needed to, but eventually we shut off the shower, helped each other dry off, and got dressed.

Another thing that was odd, but comforting. I'd spent enough time here in the past month that I had clothes here already.

"You know, you could just move in," Kenzie said casually.

Part of my mind revolted at the idea. The bit of me conditioned to not trust an offer like that. That tiny voice was already countering with, *and sleep in the guest room?*

"Bed's big enough for three." Scott's comment cut that doubt off. "As we've proven. And if it's no, we'll get a bigger bed."

"I might just be agreeable to that." I let the more confident part of me take over speaking. The bit of me that trusted them. Loved them.

Because with Scott and Kenzie, I wasn't a third wheel. I was part of them. A tricycle? Whatever we called it, the connection we all shared was wonderful.

They were family.

We ordered breakfast, and laid everything out on the table in the kitchen nook. We were about halfway through the meal when my phone rang.

Dominic. "I have to get this." I poured the apology into my voice as I pushed away from the table.

I wandered into the living room, though whatever this was, it was like I'd share it at the end of the call. "Morning," I said.

"Hey. Sorry to call you on the weekend."

"No worries." I had yet to have a bad phone call with Dominic.

"I'm hearing things through the grapevine, and I thought you might be interested, both for you and to pass along," he said.

Oh, interesting. "I'm listening."

"Your father is on the outs with his company. Apparently the press release he sent out right before SXSW was vaporware. The software he announced doesn't exist, and people are asking for it. It's about to plummet their company's worth."

Really. I may not be super business savvy, but I recognized enough to know this was horrible news for dad, and awesome news for Rinslet. No wonder it made me giddy.

"Between you and me, things are about to crumble big time for Chester Jr." Dom's tone implied this was a big secret. He was already under investigation for some money mismanagement, and that added to this is career ending."

"How do you know I think this is good news?" I asked.

He huffed. "I worked for your grandfather."

Celebrating, especially with a business associate, felt tacky. Besides, I was itching to tell Scott and Kenzie. Finally, I got to be the one who swooped in and rescued Scott. "Thank you for calling me. Let me know if you need anything from me and keep me posted?"

"I will." Dominic's smile was audible.

I disconnected and tried to keep myself contained as I headed back into the kitchen nook. I was pretty sure I failed, because Kenzie and Scott new something was up immediately.

I shared the news, and was greeted with cheers and hugs and kisses.

The kisses were probably my favorite part. From Kenzie. From Scott.

Because never in a million years would I have imagined that I could have something this incredible. Now that I did, I was never giving it up.

EPILOGUE - BRIENNE

Five years later

IT WAS ALWAYS STRANGE DIPPING MY TOES BACK INTO THE gaming world, the way I was tonight. Familiar faces filled the convention room, most of them friendly, only a few of them not.

That ratio had shifted a lot since Kenzie, Scott, and I let our relationship go public five years ago. The environment at Rinslet had reached a point where I couldn't get anything done. The whispers, the stares, and the outright hostility were too much.

It had eaten me up inside back then to deal with it, because I thought that place was perfect for me. I'd realized that was the thing I loved most about the job—it was a place where I belonged. Once I ceased to…

It had sucked to quit, Chloe wasn't happy at all. But she and I had stayed friends, which was easier now that I wasn't working for her, and I'd moved on to do similar work with Kenzie.

In the main area of the convention center now, excitement was reaching a fevered pitch. There were rumors that this was a huge announcement. That Rinslet was finally showing off what they'd been teasing for ages.

This wasn't a big convention. Judith had taken a team of people from Rinslet and started her own software company. With Elliot. With other senior members of the staff. With Scott's input and money, and with a large portion of my Grandpa's money.

And tonight they were going to show it all off publicly for the first time.

I was excited for them.

Gaming wasn't my industry anymore, though. Kenzie and I had started a different venture. We advocated for people who didn't have the knowledge or money or contacts to face the system on their own. If we ran into something we couldn't help with, Kenzie had a mile long list of contacts who were willing to step in and donate their time.

And I had more than I'd realized too. For instance, Dominic had helped Manda with the legal side of her struggles.

"Ooh, Cole's here." Kenzie's voice jarred me from my mental traipse of *previously on*. "I'm going to go say *hi*."

"Have fun." I gave her a quick kiss and squeezed her hand, and she headed into the crowds.

The Wizard—aka Cole—was before my time at Rinslet, but everyone knew the stories about the guy who did a lot of everything, and both stole Judith's heart back in the day, then let her break his when they divorced.

The worst thing I'd ever heard anyone say about him was *I can't believe the grumpy asshole left.*

I continued to watch the crowds from a distance. I'd said *hello* to everyone I cared to, and I was here for Scott, not to mingle. As the minutes ticked away, the rumble of excitement grew louder, and the words more distinct. People wondering what this was. What were they about to see? Would it live up to the hype?

It totally would. This was such a fantastic concept.

"Grand denizens of industry." A booming voice flooded the room, and Dustin stepped onto the stage. He'd been one of Rinslet's newer artists, but the man had some serious job wanderlust, and as soon as he was given the option to join AcesPlayed and make something new, he jumped on it.

Tonight he wore a T-shirt with a spade on it. Several of them had that same logo tattooed somewhere on them.

"Thank you everyone for coming out at the last minute." His confidence and presence kept everyone's eyes on him. The Rinslet logo blinked up behind him on the screen. "I'm sure you're all wondering what this is about. If you're not, I didn't do my job."

Light laughter rolled through the room.

It was almost more fun to watch his rapt audience than him, but that was mostly because I knew what was coming.

"Tonight, we're excited to introduce AcesPlayed—because we're the first and we'll continue to be the best at what we do. Most of you know our team from our time at Rinslet—previously the most awesome gaming company in the world to work for."

The image on the large screens morphed from a Rinslet logo into the spade on his shirt, with AcesPlayed beneath it. "We're going to miss our colleagues. It's been an amicable parting of ways, but we have parted regardless."

Murmurs rolled through the crowd as excitement and curiosity swelled.

Scott slid up next to me and wrapped his arm around my waist. "What do you think of the show so far?"

"Lots of hype."

"It's worth it."

I knew he was right. I'd played so many alpha versions of the game, and the people working on it were so talented.

"Tonight, we say goodbye to the people we came up in this industry with, in the most gaming way possible," Dustin said. "A little friendly competition in the game we've built. This is where you want to be recording, if you're not, because this is where I get salesy and show you something you've never seen before."

Cell phones came up, raised above heads and all pointed at Dustin. He explained this was a new kind of multiplayer RPG. It wasn't an MMO, all the servers were private, because they offered two things no one else had in this configuration.

A strictly adult only game, complete with nudity. Sex. Any sorts of hookups a person wanted, as long as it didn't break any local or federal laws. And players could either be the adventurers or the monsters.

"They're eating this up." I grinned.

Kenzie rejoined us as well, and leaned her head against my shoulder. "Of course they are. Video game history, baby."

Dustin introduced developers from each team. Rinslet would play the adventurers, and AcesPlayed were the boss monster and his add-ons.

As the teams battled back and forth, the room erupted in a wave of cheers and friendly boos. It was a close game, with dead on both sides, and stat bars in the red for anyone left standing. In the end, giant red letters flashed on the screen announcing the adventurers' party had wiped, and evil maintained its control of the valley.

Applause and boos filled the room, all good-natured.

Dustin stepped forward to take questions, but we were done here. The hype machine would continue to operate, without me, and I preferred it that way. I wouldn't hide from the attention, I wouldn't change who I was for the public eye, but I was also far happier not being a part of it.

I had something better. Five years ago, I never imagined something like this was possible. The love I had for Kenzie. For Scott. The way they returned that with an intensity and sincerity that stole my breath.

This was a better family and life than I could've ever imagined building for myself.

THANK you for riding the highs and lows with Brienne, Kenzie, and Scott.

Manda will have a book in the future, *Bury the Past*, so keep an eye on my website allysonlindt.co for details.

www.ingramcontent.com/pod-product-compliance
Lightning Source LLC
Chambersburg PA
CBHW031943240626
47153CB00003B/837